BLADE
SHADOWRIDGE GUARDIANS MC
BOOK 10

PEPPER NORTH

PHOTOGRAPHY BY
R+M PHOTOGRAPHY

COVER MODEL
JOSH LAMECH

Pepper North
With a Wink Publishing, LLC

CHAPTER
ONE

B lade backed his bike into a parking spot. With a quick, practiced movement, his boot knocked the kickstand to brace the colossal beast of a cycle he called his own. It was a rumbling testament to his skill of adding special additions to a motorcycle.

He sat there for a moment while he pulled his gloves off and unbuckled his helmet. Blade had seen too many bike accidents to risk messing up his skull. Bikers rarely came back from that type of injury. He stood, swung his leg over the bike, and grabbed a wrapped item from his saddlebag. Dropping his helmet along with his gloves into the storage area, Blade turned toward the bright blue door.

She likes color.

He'd caught a glimpse of a custom-made bolo tie holder at The Hangout last night. Not that Blade had any desire to be a cowboy wearing a string-like necklace. He was only interested in the quality of the workmanship. Steele had suggested he could have kept the guy from nearly fainting by simply asking about the decoration instead of cornering him and lifting the piece up to examine it closely. Who knew that he'd panic and almost strangle himself in his attempt to get away?

When the cowboy had regained his breath, he'd eagerly shared where he'd picked up the bolo tie. Then he'd taken off at high speed. Blade shook his head at the memory. Blade hadn't even pulled a weapon.

Shrugging, Blade walked forward toward the bright door and pushed it open. A set of bells attached to the inner handle jingled, announcing his presence. He looked around the jewelry store, which showcased unique items in a very attractive way. Earrings, bracelets, and necklaces sparkled from every display, along with jeweled pins, barrettes, and a few things Blade didn't recognize. *Yes, this is the place.*

"I'll be with you in a minute," a husky female voice called from the back.

"I'll wait," he answered. The sound alone intrigued him. What would she look like? Blade had a very specific taste in female companions. Little.

"Not that kind of Little," he said aloud, spotting a toddler peeking around the door to the backroom.

At the sound of him speaking, the child walked directly toward him. The corners of Blade's lips curved up at the sight of her pink princess dress with the ruffled skirt, sparkling waistband, and puffed sleeves. She held her hands toward Blade.

"Up!"

"Sorry, kid. I don't want your mom to get mad at me."

"Up!" she demanded with a stomp of her foot. When Blade made no move to lean over, the corners of her mouth trembled. Seconds later, a fat tear rolled down her cheek.

"Princess, you should go see your mommy," he suggested, lowering himself down to one knee.

She shook her head and walked forward to touch Blade's leather cut. The child patted it like he was a pet before poking one of the shiny snaps running down the front.

"Of course. You're out in the shop. The last place I would have thought to check," that husky voice announced.

Blade looked up to see a captivating woman with bright blue

hair and a myriad of tattoos. Her skin radiated color in countless patterns and shapes that all combined into an intriguing motif that he instantly wanted to explore closely. The woman's shape drew his attention as well—curvy, in an understated delectable way. He smiled without meaning to. She was so unique. She was also peeved.

"Kinsley, come here. How did you get out of your playpen? I've been looking for you everywhere."

Kinsley shook her head. She continued to explore Blade's cut, sliding her fingers over the worn leather. He laughed when she leaned forward to lick him.

"Kinsley. No. You don't know where that's been." She scolded the child and then paused, seemingly realizing how that must sound to Blade.

"No." The girl's response was perfectly clear and emphatic. She held on to Blade's vest and worked very hard to lift one leg to straddle and push herself up to sitting on his bent leg.

Blade steadied her as she wobbled. "Whoa, princess."

"Tank you," Kinsley answered and lifted her arms for Blade to hug her close.

To save her from tumbling, he wrapped an arm around her. Standing, he rose with Kinsley happily cuddling his chest. She laid her head on his shoulder and rubbed her cheek against the leather.

"I'm sorry. Kinsley never interacts with anyone but family. I hope she hasn't bothered you," the woman said, coming forward. She tried to lift Kinsley out of Blade's arm, but the toddler slumped back toward his chest, refusing. "No!" He obviously fascinated her.

"She's no bother. All the girls are attracted to a leather-clad biker." Blade pointed out.

The woman rolled her eyes. "She'll go to college, study law, become a lawyer, and put bad bikers in jail."

"Just as I thought, she won't be able to stay away from them," Blade teased. Enjoying this interaction more than he'd have thought possible, he wasn't in any hurry to go. He studied the woman in front of him. She'd drawn her striking blue hair into a messy bun that made him want to pull each hairpin out one by one. The daydream of her tresses tumbling down was sexy, and he pulled his thoughts back to reality.

He studiously kept his gaze from roving over her. He'd already surveyed her sweet form. Her brilliant blue eyes were spectacular, but Blade considered her plump lips to be his favorite feature. How would they feel under his?

"Ahem. I'll take Kinsley now." The woman took a step closer and reached out her hands to the child.

"No." The toddler's answer was definite.

"How about if I hold her while we do some business? By then, she'll be tired of me and ready to go back to Mom. Right, Kinsley?"

"Mom go work. An Saffire."

"That's right. Aunt Sapphire," the woman said to Kinsley before looking at him. "She's my niece. Her mom's babysitter is having a baby today. Kinsley gets to come to the shop with me for a few days."

"Ah." A few puzzle pieces in his brain clicked together. He liked kids, just hadn't considered having any of his own yet. Definitely his interest in Sapphire wasn't dampened by the thought that she was a mom, but he wouldn't choose to pursue someone with a child unless he was serious. That wasn't fair to the young one.

Blade supported Kinsley with one arm and held out the other. "I'm Blade."

"Really?" she asked, putting her hands on her hips as she looked over his body, lingering on the weapons he had secured to his form. "None of those can come loose for the baby, right?"

"Not baby." Kinsley corrected her before leaning forward to gnaw on his jacket's lapel.

"Kinsley, don't chew on the nice biker's coat. How about a

cookie?" she asked, rounding the counter to pull a box of children's animal crackers from underneath.

Kinsley held her hand out eagerly.

"She can't pull any of my weaponry," Blade assured her as
she got close once more. "What's your name?"

"Weaponry, hmm." She abandoned that line of questioning.
"I'm Sapphire Jones. The Blue Door is my store."

"Did you create this?" Blade asked, pulling the photo of the
bolo up on his phone with one hand as the little girl laid her
head on his shoulder once again as she munched on the hard
cookie.

"I made it," Sapphire said with a nod. She paused to consider
the imposing biker in front of her.

"No offense, but a bolo would look weird with the biker
thing you have going," Sapphire suggested, waving a hand
toward him.

The corners of his lips curved upward. He'd smiled more in
the last ten minutes than he had in months. He shook his head
slightly. "I like the artwork. I'm looking for an artist to add
stones to some of my knives. Would you be interested?"

She stared at him for a minute before answering. "Tell me
more."

By the time Blade showed her the hilt of a knife he was
working on and described what he had in mind, she was
intrigued. He could tell from her questions and the sketches she
started making on a pad of paper. It was obvious she enjoyed
challenges.

"Last question. Are you a jerk?"

"Nope. Pure Daddy."

"Oh. You have kids. That's why you're so good with Kinsley," Sapphire said, focusing on the now-sleeping toddler.

"No, I don't have any children." Blade controlled his expression as her gaze returned to mesh with his. He watched her
expression, hoping to see a spark of interest.

"A Daddy with no children?" Lines formed across her forehead before her stunning eyes lit up. The look of shock told him a lot. Her mouth rounded in an O as her cheeks turned a faint pink. "A Daddy Dom?"

"Through and through. Do you want to put Kinsley down for a nap? I don't think she'll wake up if you take her now," Blade suggested.

Sapphire drew closer and gently plucked Kinsley from his arms. Blade enjoyed the innocent brush of her hands against his chest and exposed skin. The contact felt electric. Her gaze met his. Her blush was endearing.

"They exist?" she blurted out.

"Daddy Doms?" he guessed. "They do."

"Oh!" With a peek over her shoulder, she escaped into the back.

An idea popped into his mind. Blade hurried outside and grabbed the teddy bear he'd driven around with for a while. Returning to the shop, he left the bear and his name and number on a slip of paper by the cash register.

Sapphire hurried back into the main shop. She'd heard the bells on the door jingle and knew there were more customers waiting for her. To her surprise, she discovered the shop was empty. He'd left?

Her heart sank in her chest. He'd just disappeared? Sapphire shook her head. She should have known better than to hope someone special had waltzed into her life.

The familiar jingle drew her attention back to the door. An older woman Sapphire quickly assessed to be a tourist walked in and looked around. "Welcome to The Blue Door. Let me know if I can help you."

"I'm searching for something special for my grandniece's birthday. Earrings maybe?"

"Tell me about her. Does she have a favorite color? What does she normally enjoy?" Sapphire asked with a smile. She loved matching customers with her creations. Her heart was happy to know her jewelry would go to someone who'd appreciate and wear it.

"Black. She's one of those teenagers who always wear that black makeup. Gloth, or something, I think is what they call it."

"Jeans? Shorts? What clothing does she like?" Sapphire didn't correct her terminology to goth. The woman obviously cared about this person in her life and was interested in finding something special.

"Short skirts with clunky boots."

"I have just the thing." Sapphire led her over to a display of chokers and ear cuffs. "These are really popular. Here's my favorite."

Picking up the beautiful pink stone on a black mesh band, Sapphire held it up to her throat. "This has a bit of color that makes pale skin gleam. It still has the dark goth allure but with a unique style. Do you think she'd like this?"

The woman reached up to run a finger over the finely smoothed metal. "This is much more comfortable than I expected. I like this."

"Would you care to try it on?"

The older woman hesitated and then nodded. "Could I?"

"Of course."

Sapphire adeptly fastened the necklace into place and gestured to the mirror on the wall. "See what you think." Her smile broadened as the woman turned this way and that, admiring it.

"I adore this. I'll take it."

"She'll love it too. I have some with a gold or silver band instead of the black. Would you like to shop for yourself? Maybe you'd enjoy one as well?"

"I prefer purple."

"I do, too. How about this silver one with amethyst beads? It's a little longer. It will sit on your collarbones instead of snug around your neck." Sapphire pointed out.

"It looks so different. Can I try this one on, too?" the woman asked with a smile.

"Let's do it," Sapphire said, enchanted by how much brighter and happier the woman seemed now compared to her appearance when she'd entered.

By the time Sapphire carried one necklace and a matching ear cuff to the cash register, the customer chatted happily as her fingers stroked over the necklace she hadn't wanted to take off. Sapphire set the items on a piece of velvet and noticed the light grey teddy bear next to the cash register. Her heart skipped a beat.

"Isn't that adorable? Is he the shop mascot?"

"No. I've never seen him before. The previous shop visitor must have left it for me." Sapphire shared her guess. Her voice must have given away her delight to find the stuffie. Her lingering dejection evaporated at the thought that Blade hadn't simply disappeared. He'd left her something a Daddy Dom would.

"It sounds like that visitor needs to come back often."

"I hope he will." Sapphire rang up the purchases as quickly as possible. All she wanted to do was hug the furry present.

CHAPTER
TWO

She almost felt bad about hiding Silver from Kinsley. Almost. When her sister dropped in to pick up her daughter, Sapphire breathed a sigh of relief. The little girl was an absolute angel when she was around, but it took a lot of energy to anticipate what she would do next in the shop full of precious items.

When The Blue Door was quiet once again, Sapphire picked up the card that she'd found on Silver's tummy. Blade. No last name. It had a motorcycle garage listed along with the logo of the Shadowridge Guardians MC. Tonight was her short day. It was almost closing time. Should she drive over with some of the designs she'd created between customers to show him? Butterflies barrel raced in her stomach.

Before she could wimp out, Sapphire texted the number.

Blade. Check these out. If you'll be at the address on the card you left at five, I'll stop by, and we can talk.

Her phone buzzed back almost immediately. *What's his name?*

She hesitated before answering. *Silver.*

I like it. I'll be here. You did good, Little girl.

. . .

Sapphire stared at the phone. Little with a capital. That couldn't be a mistake. A shiver of excitement ran down her spine. Without thinking, she picked up the stuffie and hugged it close to her chest. "Silver. I'm so scared." Did she imagine the teddy bear squeezed her back?

The last hour of the day was crazy busy. That kept Sapphire from second-guessing her decision to stop by the Guardians' shop. It helped keep her from worrying. There were still a few times she waffled back and forth.

Picking Silver up along with a file of the sketches, Sapphire double-checked that she'd locked the front door and fastened the security bars in place for the windows. She set the alarm and listened for it to beep before letting herself out the back door. Once in her car, she placed Silver on the passenger seat. Exhaling a long breath, she started toward the motorcycle repair shop.

Everyone knew the Shadowridge Guardians. Sapphire had seen them from a distance as she'd driven around town and from the windows of her shop. She'd noticed they gathered out at The Hangout some evenings, but she had never checked out the bar and grill. Going to a bar alone didn't sound like fun, and her besties from high school were married with babies. They didn't have the energy to dance the night away anymore.

Most evenings when the shop was closed and even when it was a slow night, Sapphire dreamed up designs for her jewelry. She loved matching clever settings with gems to make the final piece both a work of art and something people would treasure. Her shop was thriving and gaining a reputation for unique jewelry. That satisfied her creative side, but Sapphire often felt alone. She'd had boyfriends in the past but nothing serious.

As she negotiated the streets filled with rush hour traffic, Sapphire wondered what the inside of the motorcycle shop would look like. Would it be gritty and grimy from the oil and grease? Or would it be shiny chrome and windows?

The parking lot was partially filled with a number of cars. She wondered if this was the time when customers dropped off bikes or picked them up. Sapphire knew jewelry but absolutely nothing about motorcycles. She pulled into a space and gathered up the designs she'd worked on.

"Silver. You stay here. I don't want you to get dirty in the shop," Sapphire told her new best friend and then rolled her eyes at herself. She'd caught herself talking to the teddy bear repeatedly today.

She opened her door, stepped out, and turned to the building. She hesitated for a breath to gather her courage. It was safe in there, wasn't it? Scanning the area, she noted everyone was male without a woman in sight.

"I need someone with big biceps to pull the brake pad box down from the top shelf," a female voice called.

Instantly, Sapphire felt more at ease to walk in. Of course, it was silly, but knowing there was another woman inside made the shop less threatening. Squaring her shoulders, she headed for the door.

"Hey. Hold on a minute for me, please," the woman called.

Sapphire traced the sound to see a woman supporting a box precariously perched on the edge of an upper shelf. Without thinking, she slammed her purse and the folder on the counter before rushing to the woman's side. "Here, let me help."

Steadying one corner of the box, she looked at the employee and guessed. "I think this weighs more than both of us."

"Probably. Would you mind going into the shop to shout for one of the guys to help me?"

"I can't let go of this. It will crush you. Do you think if we yell together, someone will hear?" Sapphire asked.

"Let's try it." Under her breath, the woman mumbled, "My butt is going to be so red."

"What?" Sapphire asked.

"Sorry. Just thinking out loud. On the count of three, call help. One, two, three."

"HELP!"

Pounding footsteps sounded behind them. Sapphire glanced over her shoulders to see three large men entering.

"Fuck, Addie. Your ass is going to be on fire," a bald man with a scowl told her as he ran forward to push the box back on the shelf.

"Really, Faust? I was trying to get it down."

"Addie's going to take a short break," a stern-looking bearded biker said calmly and held out his hand. "And then she's going to practice asking for assistance ahead of time."

"Are you a new employee here?" The man Sapphire now knew as Faust asked her, distracting Sapphire from trying to figure out what was going on.

"No. I own a jewelry store downtown."

When the man's expression didn't change and he stood staring at her, Sapphire quickly added, "I just came to talk to Blade and heard her cry out." Faust just stared at her. Refusing to be intimidated by the large man, Sapphire squared her shoulders. "I'd do it again too. Girl code. We support each other."

"It's okay, Faust. That's Sapphire. She's mine."

Sapphire turned to see Blade standing in the doorway. *Oh, thank God.* She pivoted back to look at Faust and couldn't believe the change in his expression. He no longer regarded her as an interloper. His slight smile was almost gentle.

"Sorry, Sapphire." Without another word, he left.

Staring at his broad back as he disappeared, Sapphire didn't even have time to respond. Her gaze flew to meet Blade's. "Yours?" She squelched the thrill she felt at that idea. Surely, she should be offended.

"Yes. Do you mind if I finish cleaning up my area before we look at your designs? I've almost gotten everything put away. You might enjoy seeing the inside of the shop."

Distracted by that idea, she nodded. "I'd like that." Sapphire had grabbed her things from the counter before her brain computed that he'd said yes. By the time she'd whirled back around, he disappeared through the doorway. Walking quickly, she followed him.

"Blade, I don't think...." Sapphire's mouth snapped closed as she entered the work area. All the bikers turned to look at her.

"Blade's in the last work bay. Stay between the painted lines," Faust told her softly before addressing the others in a louder tone, "She's his." The bikers all nodded and called polite greetings.

What is going on here? Shaking her head, Sapphire walked down the aisle he'd pointed out.

The space was divided into different sections. Even to her untrained eye, she could see that each area had a particular focus. Spotting Blade, she hurried to his side. Unable to resist, she scanned his hard body. Blade had a physical job, but he obviously worked out as well. His powerful ass and thighs alone screamed he'd done a million squats.

"Everyone thinks we're together," she hissed, forcing herself to focus.

Blade looked around and answered, "We are."

"Not like in the same space. They think we're together-together."

"I can live with that. Here. I've cleaned off my bench. Set the sketches here," Blade said as he turned on a light on the surface.

She stared at the devastatingly handsome man and didn't budge. "Why did you say I was yours?"

"Have you ever had that knowledge deep in your gut that something was right? Like an interview for a position you were confident you'd enjoy, or an apartment that feels happy?"

"Of course. What does that have to do with anything?" Why was he talking about places to live or jobs?

"I've looked for my Little girl for a long time. I'm sure I've found her," Blade said, holding her gaze with his. His voice was quiet. In the noisy environment, she knew only she could hear him.

Sapphire took a step forward. "I'm not even positive I'm a

Little girl," she whispered. Her heart pounded so loudly, she wondered if he could hear it. Her emotions flip-flopped between excitement and fright.

"Then we figure it out together," he suggested, moving closer. He reached a hand out to smooth over her hair before tangling his fingers in the locks at the base of her skull. Blade tightened his grip, and Sapphire tilted her head back to ease the tug on her hair.

Blade slowly lowered his mouth to hers. She had what felt like a lifetime to stop him and didn't even consider shifting away. When his lips met hers in a soft kiss, she rose on her tiptoes to press her mouth against his. Something drew her to him.

He wrapped his free arm around her waist, guiding her forward. The design sheets crinkled, crumpled between them.

Damn, this man can kiss. Sapphire abandoned herself to the pleasure he cultivated. The long slow kisses wiped every thought from her mind. When he deepened the kiss, she moaned into his mouth. He tasted like peppermint-flavored masculinity. Suddenly, her favorite flavor shifted from chocolate to sweet mint.

When he lifted his head, a small sound slipped through her lips. Without consciously meaning to, Sapphire lifted her fingers to her lips as she stared at him in wonder.

"I know, Little girl. I feel it too. You're mine until you decide our relationship doesn't work for you. I'm hoping that never happens."

"I'm not sure how to be Little."

"Can you be brave for Daddy?" he asked.

"Daddy?"

"Being Little takes being true to yourself and trying different things to find what makes you happy. I'll be with you every step of the way," Blade promised.

"We just met each other," she protested. She should move away from him, but she didn't want to.

"I think we've already figured out the most important details, right?" he asked and brushed her hair away from her face.

Sapphire nodded.

"Door going down," a loud voice announced. The open bay doors crept toward the floor with a metallic rattle.

Realizing where they were, Sapphire stepped back. Blade tightened his arm around her and then released her as if he were reluctant to let her go. "I forgot they were here," she whispered. "What are they going to think of me?"

"You're mine. That's all that matters. The Shadowridge Guardians take care of their own," he told her in a very definite tone before changing the subject. "Show me your designs."

"Oh." She raised the sheets and walked to the workspace he'd indicated before to set them out. Sapphire held her breath as Blade scanned all the images closely.

"I like how you colored these in instead of just noting the stones. That makes it easier to imagine. These are incredible. You skirted the line between attractive and too girly perfectly."

"Could you show me where these are going?" Sapphire asked.

"I can put blades in several places on a bike. How much do you know about motorcycles?"

"Pretend I'm a total novice," Sapphire answered. She wanted to hear what he would tell her. Besides, she wasn't an expert. She'd just ridden on the back of a bike, holding onto her art school boyfriend. Like her previous love interests, he hadn't lasted too long. Heavens knew he wasn't a Daddy. Was that what made Blade so exciting?

A smile spread Blade's lips, and he brushed away a wavy lock of deep brown hair that always seemed to be in his face. "Let me show you."

He linked his fingers with hers like it was something they always did and led Sapphire over to the cycle sitting a short distance away. Blade rubbed a hand over the large, rounded part in front of the seat. "This is the tank. It holds gasoline to fuel the bike."

"I knew that," Sapphire assured him.

"I can add throwing stars to snap into place on the tank." He twisted his wrist and removed a metal star with sharpened edges.

"I thought that was part of the design. Those come off?" She stared at the metal piece before examining the spot where he'd disguised it. "Isn't that sharp?" Sapphire asked, reaching a finger out to touch the gleaming edge.

"This isn't a toy. It will slice you," Blade warned, pulling it away and snapping it back into place. "See how it locks onto the tank, so the metal covers the sharpened sections?"

"That's a perfect disguise. I'd never think it was a weapon."

"Adding gems would throw the balance off on the star or I'd have you design something to embellish it," Blade said, running his fingers over the device.

"Why would you need that?" she asked.

"There are people that don't like bikers. Road rage is crazy. Some motorcycle clubs protect their turf physically. And there are bad people out in the world. Do you have something in your car in case of a problem?"

"No. I know I couldn't throw that. I'd end up dropping that star on my foot or flipping it back to get me in the shoulder." Sapphire laughed.

"A star is not the weapon I'd give you. I'm sure we can find something for protection that matches your abilities and style," Blade told her.

"I'm not weaving knives into my T-shirt, Blade. It's a look that works for you and that leather vest," she said, waving a hand toward his cut, which had been hung carefully on a hook.

"How heavy is that thing?" Sapphire turned to consider his powerful shoulders and knew it didn't matter. He'd never notice five or ten pounds of weapons.

When her gaze rose to his face, she discovered him smiling broadly. "Do I amuse you?"

"Yes. In a good way, of course. What are you doing tonight?" Blade asked.

"Bringing you the designs."

"I approve them all. I'll load your trunk with some unsharpened knives for you to embellish," Blade told her. "Keep track of your time and supplies so I can pay you. Don't work cheap. I'll pass along the cost to the customer."

"I'll be honest," she assured him.

"Of course you will. If not, I'll spank your bottom crimson."

All the rest he said after that went right over her head. The arousal already shimmering inside her at simply being close to Blade exploded into a fire at the thought of him paddling her. A visual image of being stretched over his hard thighs popped into her brain, pushing any coherent thoughts from her mind. He might as well have been speaking in Greek. She just watched his handsome face and let the words float over her head. When he stopped, she grabbed frantically at the last thing she heard. Pizza? Chinese?

"I'm starving."

"Then, let's go. Have you ridden on a motorcycle before?"

"When I was in college," she admitted.

"Perfect. Let's go."

Sapphire nodded automatically and took his hand when he extended it. Inside, she marveled at how easy everything felt with Blade—like they'd known each other for weeks. Had she ever felt this excited about any man? Not a chance.

CHAPTER
THREE

Riding with Blade was unlike her previous experience. She relaxed against his honed body and mirrored his actions. What made this so different from riding with that other guy in art school? She'd gotten so tense each time she'd perched on his bike that she'd been sore when they got anywhere. Bouncing along with him quickly became something she dreaded.

Smooth, exhilarating, and yummy. That was how she felt wrapped around Blade. Well, yummy referred to his scent. Blade smelled like polish and fire from his work, but underlying that simmered hot, spicy male. Sapphire could roll around in that and be happy. An instant flash of what making love with Blade would be like popped into her brain. She bit her lip at the surge of pure hunger that filled her.

"He might make me stand on my head."

"What?" Blade asked, looking quickly over his shoulder.

"Nothing. Just thinking of my weekly yoga class." Sapphire covered for herself while mentally whacking her forehead for talking aloud.

"I've never tried yoga. Where do you go?"

"I watch it on TV. That's the easiest." She invented an excuse. *Hey, quick thinking.*

She tightened her hold on Blade as he slowed to turn into the parking lot of The Hangout. He drove around the back and parked with a line of motorcycles. Sapphire smiled to see several bikes had colorful helmets. She wanted to see the bikers wearing those.

"Slide off, Little girl."

"Oh, sorry. I was looking at all the helmets."

"You'll enjoy meeting the special women who rode in with my brothers." Blade predicted, throwing his leg over the bike in a practiced move.

"Your brothers," Sapphire repeated. "Are there more of your gang here?"

"Motorcycle club, Blue Eyes. Not a gang," he corrected.

Shrugging, Sapphire wondered what the difference was. MC club, gang? They seemed the same to her. Maybe the temperament of the members was the distinguishing factor.

"Come on. Are you hungry? They have amazing trash-can nachos here," Blade suggested as he took off his helmet.

"Extra jalapeños?"

"If that's what you would like," he said, walking forward to unfasten her helmet. "Which helmet do you like the best?"

"I like this blue one you found for me," Sapphire answered quickly, keeping her gaze away from the one with fuzzy pink decorations.

"I'm glad. You know there are ways to personalize it. Angel wings. Tattoo designs. Even ears."

Her eyes widened at the mention of that last one. When he smiled, she quickly said, "Oh, it's fine by itself."

"So, ears, huh? Do you want fuzzy ones like Elizabeth has? Those are hers over there," he pointed to the exact embellishments Sapphire had coveted.

"Really, it's not necessary to decorate my helmet. I won't ride with you that often."

"Sure, you will. I enjoyed having you curled around me. Did you enjoy the trip here?" he asked, watching her carefully.

Sapphire couldn't lie to those big brown eyes that seemed to see so much. "Yes. I loved it."

"Then we get you some blue, fuzzy ears. Or would you rather have pink?"

"Blue!" she blurted and realized that she'd just admitted she coveted the additions.

"You've got them. I'll order them tomorrow morning. Now, nachos?"

Nodding, she couldn't help bouncing on her toes in excitement. Those blue ears would be so cute. She held on to his hand when he threaded his fingers with hers and followed him to the back entrance.

Several women flirted with Blade as they walked by. Sapphire glared at them before catching herself. She shouldn't feel so territorial about a man who she'd just met. It wasn't like they were a couple or something. *He wants to be your Daddy. That's pretty serious.*

She glanced up at Blade to judge his reaction to the women's interest and found him studying her. "Did I do something wrong?"

"I'm here with you, Little girl. No one else."

"It's scary how you know what I'm thinking."

"What?" he asked, leaning closer like he couldn't hear over the music.

"It's scary...." The rest of her repeated statement disappeared as his lips pressed against hers in a quick, hard kiss that left her craving more.

"Ready to go meet everyone?" he asked as she tried to recover.

Sapphire would have agreed with anything he asked at that moment. When he tugged her hand gently, she followed him to a back corner of the large bar and grill. She hesitated, seeing a couple dancing on the floor that put everyone to shame. Blade stopped and watched with her.

"That's Talon and Elizabeth."

"He's a Shadowridge Guardian?" she asked, glancing back at Blade.

"He is. Come on. You can meet them when this song ends."

As they approached, Sapphire saw a dozen men in the MC's cut. They had claimed several tables in a partially secluded area. A number of women mingled with them. Sapphire noted a difference between the flirtatious ones trying to pick up a biker and those she guessed were already attached to a Shadowridge Guardian.

"Blade," called a blonde dressed in a short bubble skirt and lacy socks. The woman's eyes dropped to their intertwined hands and then she scanned Sapphire.

As everyone turned to look at them, Sapphire stood proudly with her shoulders back, waiting to see the group's reaction to her blue hair and tattoos. She'd always been artistic and liked things a bit out there—more colorful and her own relaxed style. From this group of bikers, she didn't expect the dismissive or scornful backlash she got from the general public. To her relief, they all seemed pleased to see them. Even the tall grumpy-looking guy who'd helped her with the box.

Sapphire was amazed when the blonde who'd greeted them rushed forward to hug her. Shocked, she allowed the contact, not knowing what else to do. She glanced over the woman's shoulder at Blade.

"Sapphire, this hugging machine is Harper. Harper, this is Sapphire." Blade introduced the two.

"What a perfect name! Your eyes are gorgeous. You're with Blade?" Harper asked.

"Thanks. Umm, yes?" Sapphire offered hesitantly.

"She's mine," Blade answered in a much more definitive tone. "We're getting some food. Are you hungry, Harper?"

"For nachos," the woman answered, batting her eyelashes at Blade.

Sapphire couldn't help but laugh. There was no real flirtation happening. She was playing Blade hard.

"I'm familiar with your vampy ways, Harper. I'm going to order nachos for Sapphire to try. Want to check with the other... others if they want to join us?" Blade asked. "Oh, and ask Doc if you can have some to eat."

Sapphire suspected that he'd changed what he'd started to say.

"Okay!" Harper agreed. The petite woman ran off to talk to a man leaning against the wall, who watched them closely.

"Other what?" she asked Blade. She could tell from his expression that he knew exactly what she was asking.

"There are some things that are best shared by the individual," he answered cryptically.

"Hmm." While Sapphire approved of him not gossiping, a part of her wanted the information he'd chosen not to reveal. She crossed her fingers hoping to get the scoop soon.

Sapphire watched as Harper's fellow slowly nodded before saying something to her. Immediately, the other woman smiled and ran over to a cluster of people seated at the table. As Harper talked to them, the entire group turned to look at Sapphire.

"Tell me they're friendly," Sapphire said out of the corner of her mouth to Blade.

"I have weapons. You're safe," he assured her as the group leapt to their feet. Two chairs clattered to the ground as four women rushed toward them.

Blade stepped in front of Sapphire and held up a hand. "Whoa, ladies."

"Oh, sorry. We didn't mean to frighten her," one assured Blade.

"I'm not scared," Sapphire told them as she peeked over the biker's broad shoulder. She couldn't move around him. Blade held her hand pressed to his firm butt. She struggled not to explore his body.

"We'll be good," Harper promised.

Blade relented and stepped back to Sapphire's side. "Everyone wants nachos?"

"And to meet Sapphire," a young woman dressed all in black confessed.

"Say hello and then go ask your... men for permission," Blade instructed.

Sapphire watched in amazement as they lined up in front of her. In three minutes, she'd met Harper's friends, Remi, Eden, Carlee, and Molly. They were super sweet and seemed happy to meet her.

Molly lingered after greeting her. "Elizabeth is here too. She's out dancing. Talon's teaching us a few steps. It's so much fun. Look, here they come."

The couple arrived in excellent spirits. It was easy to see that they enjoyed dancing together. The woman zeroed in on Sapphire immediately as a new arrival and introduced herself. "Hi, I'm Elizabeth."

"Hi, Elizabeth. I'm Sapphire. The two of you dance superbly."

"Talon can make anyone appear good."

"That's two, Little girl."

That quiet comment drew Sapphire's attention to the handsome man at Elizabeth's side. His face was serious as he focused on the other woman.

"I'm smart, and my friends love me," Elizabeth added to the conversation. Then, as if she realized that was random, she clarified for Sapphire. "Daddy makes me think of two nice things about myself if I say anything negative."

"That's wonderful. I'll tell you one more. I think you're an excellent dancer," Sapphire added.

Elizabeth looked at Talon and then back at Sapphire. "Thank

you. I love to move to the music. It's so much fun. Hey, everyone's putting the tables together."

"I'm ordering nachos. Are you hungry, Elizabeth?" Blade asked.

"Starving! No jalapeños for me," she requested.

"I'll put in a couple of orders. One with jalapeños and one without," Blade promised. "Elizabeth, would you help Sapphire find a seat?"

"Of course. Let's join the others. You've met everyone?" Elizabeth asked as she walked with Sapphire over to the table.

"Yes. They're all nice."

"They're the best friends I've ever had. You'll see," Elizabeth assured her.

The thought that she'd like to have people in her life she felt that close to resonated in Sapphire's mind. She'd always had friends, but they'd been more acquaintances. These women appeared bonded. Their body language proved that as they leaned close to each other with happy expressions.

"Jalapeño lovers on that side. Sane people over here," Harper directed.

The two women looked at each other and split up. Sapphire sat down on the spicy section, struggling to remember the two women's names. The flurry of introductions had evaporated from her mind.

"Yay! You live on the edge like Carlee and me," said the dark-haired goth-like woman, pointing to the cutie with pigtails.

Whew! That was one name. Carlee and....

"Remi really doesn't like peppers, but they seem daring, so she tries to eat them. Her Daddy devours them all for her." Carlee exposed the truth and reminded Sapphire of the previous speaker's name.

"She's right. I'm a wimp," Remi agreed.

"Daddy? You're not...." Sapphire didn't want to label them with something they weren't.

"Little? I can only talk about myself. I am. Kade's my Daddy.

He's the biker with the most tattoos. I love yours. Does this mean something?" Remi said, skillfully changing the subject as she pointed to a sun design on Sapphire's inner wrist.

"That's my everlasting summer. I didn't enjoy school much when I was a kid. Well, nothing other than art class and then art school later on. I designed that one when I graduated from high school to celebrate that I didn't have to struggle anymore," Sapphire told her.

"School can be hard," Carlee agreed. "My Daddy is so good with numbers. He's an accountant."

This time, Sapphire didn't ask. She followed Carlee's gaze to a handsome man who played pool.

"Is that him, taking the shot?" Sapphire asked.

"Yes! That's Atlas," Carlee confirmed

"It's fun to see who goes with which biker," Sapphire shared.

"Which one do you think is Molly's?" Remi asked, pointing to the demurely dressed woman with glasses.

"Hmmm." Sapphire waited for Molly to give it away by glancing at one of the men. She did not. Taking a wild guess, Sapphire said, "How about the bald guy over there with the snarly look on his face? Faust?"

"She got another one," Elizabeth crowed. "You are good. They're together."

"Do me next. I'm Eden," a red-haired woman volunteered. She almost danced in her chair with excitement.

"Hmm. Opposites attract. How about that guy with the salt and pepper beard over there?" Sapphire pointed.

Eden's jaw dropped. "How did you know? That's Gabriel. He's mine."

"Honestly?" Sapphire paused. "He keeps checking on you."

The whole group turned to look at the silver fox and found his attention squarely on Eden. There was a collective gasp, and everyone swiveled to stare at Sapphire.

"You're good," Eden complimented.

"Thanks. I'm good at reading people. It comes in handy in my business."

"What do you do?" Elizabeth asked.

"I have a jewelry shop downtown."

"I noticed your earrings. I love them," Harper chimed in. "They're so unique."

"Thank you. I designed and created them," Sapphire said as she ran her fingers over the teardrop form of twisted metal dotted with small turquoise and topaz stones. They were one of her favorites because they went with a lot of colors.

"Does that ear thing hurt?" Carlee asked.

"The cuff?" Sapphire touched the gold metal band that fit on her ear. When Carlee nodded, she added, "It doesn't. It fits loosely on the cartilage of your ear. Would you like to try it?"

"Is that okay?" Carlee asked.

"Of course. It's just like sliding on someone's ring," Sapphire explained as she pulled it off. She handed it to Carlee who started to put it on and bobbled it. She looked down at her empty hand in horror. All the women pushed back their chairs and searched on the floor.

"I'm so sorry," Carlee babbled, repeating the phrase numerous times before dropping to her knees.

Everyone joined her, including Sapphire. "It's okay, Carlee."

"We don't have much time before they get suspicious. Sapphire, we're all Littles. It's okay if you aren't, but we're not good at pretending. Can we be friends?"

"I'd like that more than anything," Sapphire answered. A genuine smile curved the end of her lips as she met the gaze of each woman. They were lovely women, inside and out.

"In that case," Carlee lifted a hand above the table they crouched under, "I found it!"

The women peeked over the top to see the cuff sitting in the middle of her palm.

"Oh, thank goodness," Elizabeth said. "That was too precious to lose." She turned away from the bikers to wink theatrically at the others, who slowly rose to retake their seats.

"They're up to something," Faust announced in a voice that carried.

As if operating with one mind, each of the woman completely ignored that statement. Sapphire couldn't help the corners of her lips from turning up as Carlee returned her ear cuff. Already she adored this crew. They were honest, fun-loving, and open.

Most of all, they accepted her whether or not she fit with the group perfectly. She understood that they'd wanted to know if they could be themselves around her. Crossing her fingers, she hoped they understood she wasn't ever going to criticize someone for living their truth. Maybe they would tell her more about being Little?

Remi patted her leg when the conversation swirled around them again. "We're glad Blade found you."

"I'm glad I found her, too." Blade's deep voice rang out above her. "Are you all ready for nachos? Here they come!"

The men hustled to grab drinks for their Littles as the two servers carried immense trays to the table. In a practiced move, the waitresses fitted the tray over the bucket-sized garbage can and flipped it over. Lifting the metal can up, the employees allowed the layers of chips and goodies to cascade over the tray. It smelled incredible.

"Enjoy!"

"Dig in, Sapphire. I'll go grab you a drink. What goes best with nachos in your opinion?" Blade asked.

"I'll take a beer. Something light," Sapphire requested.

"You got it."

When he came back with a Mexican pale ale with a lime on the top, she knew he was a keeper. The attention he gave her felt incredible. She liked being the center of his attention.

The men pulled chairs up to the table and joined the group. The good-natured ribbing between them told Sapphire that the

Shadowridge Guardians were close. They really were a brotherhood.

She relaxed and found herself leaning against Blade's hard body. When he leaned in to kiss her temple, she smiled up at him.

"I like your people," she told him.

"That's good, because I enjoy having you here." He wrapped an arm around her waist and lifted her onto his lap.

When she shifted to slide off his muscular thighs, he asked, "Are you uncomfortable?"

"No." She shook her head.

"Then stay. I like holding you."

Wild horses couldn't have pulled her away. A hopping song and peer pressure made her join everyone on the dance floor an hour later. Sapphire discovered that kissing wasn't the only thing Blade did well. Her mind drifted to fantasize about what else he was so skilled at, and she tripped over her own feet. Her cheeks flamed hot with embarrassment.

"Whatever that thought is, I want to hear it later," Blade growled into her ear.

"Not going to happen, biker boy," she sassed back.

"We'll see about that. Slow song. Come here. I need to wrap my arms around you, Blue Eyes."

CHAPTER
FOUR

W e don't have to go," she protested when all the matched couples began to gather their things.

"You need sleep, Blue Eyes. We'll come back here again soon."

"But...."

"No buts," he interrupted. "It's time for Little girls to be in bed."

"You know I usually am awake until midnight at least," she answered, rolling her eyes.

"That stops now. Come on."

Blade lifted her off his lap and stood to hold her hand. Falling in behind the couples leaving, he escorted her out the back door and to his bike.

Sapphire watched the other men fastening the helmets on their women. They really did take care of them. She blinked up at Blade when he fit her protective gear in place as well. She'd always handled everything herself. It was a treat to have someone making sure she was safe.

"I can't wait to see the fuzzy ears on this," he told her as he secured the chin strap.

"Am I going to be on your bike enough to be worth that cost?" she asked, probing for information.

"Yes, Sapphire. There will be many opportunities for you to ride with me. You enjoyed the trip here?"

"Yeah. It was fun. I like the air whizzing around me," she told him, deliberately leaving out how much she'd loved hanging on to him.

"Perfect."

In a few minutes, they were off. The trip back to the Guardians' complex sizzled even more now. Holding onto his hard body was a complete turn-on. She'd had to struggle not to rub her breasts against his muscular back on the way. Was he as into her as she was to him?

When he stopped next to her car, she slid off the seat and moved back so he could throw his leg over after setting the kickstand. Capturing her gaze, he unfastened his helmet and set it on the seat. As he stalked forward, Sapphire felt a bit like prey. That reaction might have been threatening, but it wasn't. The simmering arousal that had brewed inside her from being so close to Blade all night seemed to flare into a bonfire. She stepped forward and lifted her mouth.

Blade pressed a quick kiss to her lips before telling her, "Let's get this helmet off so I can kiss you properly."

He made quick work of the buckle and slid the protective gear away. Blade smoothed her hair back from her face. "You are so beautiful, Blue Eyes."

"Show me this isn't crazy, Blade."

He didn't need further encouragement. Blade drew her face to his and kissed her—slow, drugging exchanges that did funny things to her stomach. Sapphire stepped closer, pressing her body to his. She loved the feel of his steely muscles supporting her and the seductive heat that built between them. He cupped her bottom with one large hand and pulled her pelvis closer to him.

"Blade," she moaned against his lips.

"Daddy, Blue Eyes."

"Daddy," she whispered, wanting to please him. It was funny what using that name did to her inside. She had fantasized for so long about having such a dominant, yet caring relationship.

The kiss that followed seared her mind with the intensity of the emotions it drew from her. When he stepped back, she clutched at his cut.

"I'm not going to make love to you for the first time in the parking lot, Sapphire. It's time for Little girls to be in bed. I'll follow you to your place."

Her mind raced. Did he plan to make love to her in the parking lot later? Wait, he was coming home with her? "Will you stay?"

"Not tonight. I want you to decide to take this big step with your brain and your heart. I won't walk away from you after you're mine. You need to decide whether you can handle a motorcycle weaponist tomorrow and the next forty years."

"You want to be with me for that long?" Her heart lurched in her chest at the thought that he wanted that type of commitment.

"Plus a few more decades if we're lucky. Come on. Let's get you in your car," Blade told her as he wrapped an arm around her back to guide Sapphire to the driver's door.

"I almost forgot. I brought you some knives to work on," he jogged back to his bike and grabbed a wrapped bundle from his saddlebags. "Pop your trunk. They can stay in there until you get to the shop tomorrow. There's no edge on them."

Blade rewarded her for following his directions with another kiss before he pulled his helmet back on and straddled his bike. The roar of the motorcycle sent a shiver through her. Everything about this man was arousing.

Seeing his headlight in her rearview mirror on the way home made her indescribably happy. People spotted her blue hair and tattoos and assumed Sapphire was a lot tougher than she actually felt. Blade wasn't fooled by her outward persona. He saw her.

A few minutes later, she flipped the lights on and off to let him know she was in her apartment, safe and sound. He sat there as she pulled the blinds, watching as if he wanted to capture the last glimpses of her. Sapphire heard the rumble of his motor as he headed out. She hugged Silver to her chest, missing the alluring biker already.

Opening her eyes the next morning, Sapphire automatically checked the time. Finding she had a few minutes to laze in bed, she grabbed Silver and hugged him to her chest. She'd gotten an amazing night of sleep. She'd expected to toss and turn, but after showering and treating her body to a few orgasms thanks to her trusty vibrator, she'd crashed hard.

Sapphire bit her lip. She had this feeling that Blade wouldn't be pleased if he found out she'd pleasured herself last night. "He probably jerked off," she whispered aloud. Silver stared at her with big, scandalized eyes.

"Don't tell him, Silver. That's a secret he never needs to know."

Grinning at her silliness, Sapphire set Silver carefully aside and sat up. She headed for the bathroom and returned a few minutes later to see Silver staring at her. "What? He doesn't need to know."

The stuffed bear simply eyed her with a blank expression. Silver didn't seem to be swayed by her words.

Quickly, she ducked into her closet and pulled on a pair of jeans and a top. She hesitated there for a minute and dug out some high-top sneakers that would be comfortable at work. The sound of her phone ringing sent her running back into the bedroom.

Grabbing her phone, she answered, "This is Sapphire."

"Something told me to call this morning. Are you okay?" Blade's deep voice sounded concerned.

Sapphire turned to glance at the teddy bear, who now wore a very innocent expression. She shook her head at the stuffie. They were going to have a long talk when she got off the phone. "I'm fine, thank you. Did you sleep well?"

"Lonely, but I slept. When do you close the shop tonight?"

"It's a late night for me. I usually am out of there at 9:30-ish," she told him.

"I'll bring dinner when I'm done in the shop."

"You don't have to do that." Sapphire rushed to assure him as she twirled a lock of hair around her fingers.

"I want to spend some time with you. If you're busy, I will be glad to wait until you have a break," he promised.

She really wanted to see him. Knowing he felt the same way made her day sparkle. "I'd like to see you."

"Me, too, Little girl."

When he hung up, she stared at her phone. Could it really be that easy to find someone who cared about her? There had to be something wrong with Blade. Sure, he was in a motorcycle club and had lots of weapons all over his body. But Blade was unique. Special.

Sapphire looked at the blue hair wrapped around her fidgeting finger. She liked uncommon things and people. There were so many layers to Blade. Heaven knew she'd never expected to meet a Daddy Dom like those in the books she read. His outward demeanor was lethal, but he was so gentle with her. And with Kinsley. Her niece had fallen in love with him immediately.

Kinsley! Oh, crap! Her niece would stay with her again today. She had to get to the shop early for the pass off or her sister would be late for work. Yanking on her shoes, she grabbed her keys and ran for the door. Her customers wouldn't care if she had makeup on.

Blade's coming. Double crap. She threw herself into the driver's

seat and started the car. He'd have to deal with her as a plain
Jane. That could make this relationship short. Sapphire
smoothed a hand over her hair as she drove out of the parking
lot. Had she even brushed her hair? Sapphire grabbed the emergency scrunchie she kept wrapped around her gear shift and
gathered the tumble of silken strands into a messy bun. That
would solve that problem.

Her sister's car was in front of the shop as she passed to go to
the back parking lot where she kept her car. She was in for it
now. Rushing through the shop, Sapphire opened the front door.
"Hi, Kinsley. Sorry, Sis."

"Bring him to the barbecue this weekend," Ellen said,
handing over the diaper bag and carrying her daughter inside.

Sapphire rolled her eyes. Her sister always picked up on
clues. She obviously thought Sapphire had just rolled out of bed
after an evening of sex. *If only.*

"I didn't really plan to come to the gathering. And there's no
him. I forgot I was watching Kinsley and needed to be here
early."

"You'll be there. I don't want to handle the cousins without
you. Now you owe me one." Her sister's slightly lighter blue
eyes twinkled.

"Wait. I'm watching Kinsley. Doesn't that mean we're even?"
Sapphire asked, amazed how her sister could always make
herself come out on top of any debate. Two years separated
them, but they'd been fast friends all their lives.

"Please. I really do want you there. And I have to meet the
new guy in your life," her sister told her before kissing her
daughter's cheek. "You be good for Aunt Sapphire."

The toddler nodded with a serious look before turning to
hold her hands out to Sapphire.

Who could resist that cute move?

Sapphire plucked Kinsley out of Ellen's arms. After kissing
her niece's sweet-smelling hair, she relented, "Fine. I'll be there.

I'm not bringing Blade." Instantly, she regretted telling her sister his name. Now, she knew he existed.

"Yes, you are. Now, I have to meet him. Blade? The cousins are going to love that name. Tell me he rides a huge motorcycle and wears leather."

"Go to work. I'm not promising anyone will be there but me." Sapphire shooed her sister out of the shop, laughing.

After setting Kinsley down to explore the shop while she got organized for the day, Sapphire couldn't keep her mind on her everyday tasks. A certain biker kept ricocheting into her thoughts. "Enough already. Stop thinking about Blade."

"Blade!" Kinsley repeated.

Sapphire stopped and looked at her. "He waved his magic wand around you too, huh?"

A babble of sounds and excited nods confirmed Kinsley's agreement. "Blade!" she repeated. "Majik!"

A mental image of what the handsome man's "magic wand" could look like popped into her mind, and she tried to control her expression in front of the child. There was no way all that raw masculinity came with a small cock. Just his natural swagger told you Blade knew a few things. And the way he'd moved on the dance floor last night. *No drooling.*

The bells at the door rang. Both Kinsley and Sapphire turned to see the object of their conversation standing framed in the doorway. The sun glistened off his brown hair, scattered over his broad shoulders. His dark eyes met hers in an intense gaze that sent a thrill through her. Blade held two cups of iced coffee and a pastry bag.

Kinsley ran toward him with her arms raised. A foot away, she tripped over her own shoes and tumbled toward the floor. Without missing a beat, Blade set one cup on the wooden floorboards as he scooped the toddler into his strong arms. "Whoa, rocket girl. You just about crashed."

Unperturbed by the close call, Kinsley immediately returned to her favorite hobby of petting Blade's leather cut. Blade let her play and held the cup and bag still in his hand to Sapphire. "Did you miss breakfast, Blue Eyes?"

"I don't know how you got my mental 'I'm starving and need caffeine' message, but thank you." Collecting the two items from him, she moved closer and kissed him lightly.

Kinsley protested and pressed a hand against Sapphire's shoulder to push her away.

Sapphire laughed and winked at Blade. "I think someone thinks you're her boyfriend."

"What a shame. I'm already taken," Blade told Kinsley sadly.

"Taken, huh?" Sapphire said, comically waggling her eyebrows to make the child laugh.

"Definitely," he assured her with a steamy look that almost made her forget where they were.

Sapphire sipped the iced coffee in her hand. It was strong and sweet. Just like she enjoyed it. "I needed this."

"Eat, too."

The stern tone of his voice made her nod in agreement. "Wait. I thought you were bringing me dinner tonight."

"I am. I stopped to have breakfast with you too."

"Oh!" Feeling selfish for leaving his coffee on the floor while she sipped away, Sapphire set her items on the workbench and retrieved his coffee for him.

"Thanks, sweetheart."

"You're welcome. I'm never here this early. Ellen, my sister, needs to fight rush hour traffic into work."

"Ah, yes. The rat race. I'll have to get to the shop soon as well. The place is swarming with nine-to-fivers who need to drop off their bikes before work."

"Don't you have to be there?" Sapphire asked.

"To have me customize their rides, customers have to come in for a consult where we decide what they need and how to add to their bike. Once we have that ironed out, they can drop their bike off before their place on the schedule," Blade shared.

"So, if I went out and bought a moped today, you could trick it out this week?"

"No, Blue Eyes. First, I don't put weapons on mopeds," he said with a shudder. "Second, I'm booked through the end of the year."

"That's months away!"

"Yes."

She stared at him. He answered like it was completely normal that his work was so treasured that people lined up for months and would wait to have him weaponize their bikes. "That's amazing, Blade. As an artist, I'll have to admit I'm jealous to my core. I would love to have people who wanted me to create something unique for them."

"You do that for people every day. My jobs are just bigger and take longer," he stated with a serious look.

"I'm honestly so excited to have a chance to bling out a bike. That's something I would never have thought of doing."

"I'm glad to have a partner in crime. Eat your breakfast, Blue Eyes. And you," he said, focusing on Kinsley, "You be a very good girl today, or I'll spank your aunt for every mess you make."

"What? That's not fair," Sapphire protested, setting her coffee down and scooping Kinsley into her arms.

When the toddler fussed at being separated from Blade, Sapphire bounced her on her hip. "You're fine. It's just us girls at the shop today. No boys allowed."

Kinsley pushed her bottom lip out as she considered the obvious unattractiveness of that decision.

Blade stepped close to Sapphire and kissed Kinsley on her temple before pressing a passionate kiss to Sapphire's lips. "Be good, Little girl." He chuckled when both females nodded. "I'll see you tonight, Blue Eyes."

"See you soon... Daddy." Sapphire loved the heat that blazed in his brown eyes. His reaction was unmistakable. Blade was a Daddy Dom through and through.

"You owe me for saying that now when I can't celebrate with you as I wish to," Blade told her as he walked to the door. His gaze meshed with hers before he closed the door behind him.

"Whoo, Kinsley. Is it hot in here or is it just me?" Sapphire asked, fanning herself. She laughed when the toddler mimicked her movement. "Thanks, Kinsley. We girls need to stick together. Let's get you some juice, and we'll split the goodie in the bag."

Sapphire turned and caught an image of herself smiling in the mirrors behind the displays. What an amazing way to start the day. Blade made her feel special.

CHAPTER
FIVE

"A barbecue, hmm?" Blade asked that evening as they shared a pizza between customers.

He'd waltzed in with one and seated himself comfortably on a stool at her workbench. He'd also made several sales for her when he'd weighed in on customer selections. Having an attractive and dangerous-looking man tell you to get both because they both are perfect on you seemed to have more power than Sapphire's opinion. She was having a great sales night. Plus, she got to spend time with Blade.

"You don't have to go if you don't want to. I understand. It's intimidating meeting someone's family," Sapphire told him. She didn't expect him to go with her. It was too soon. Sapphire had worried about asking him all day, but her sister would sense if Sapphire had chickened out.

Blade shook his head. "You're good, but I'm not manipulatable. We both know I'm not intimidated by the thought of meeting your grandmother."

"Oh, my grandmother is lovely. She's like that kindergarten teacher who everyone loved in school. It's my cousins you have to watch out for."

"I can handle your cousins," he assured her.

"Maybe regular cousins, but these two have their PhDs in belittling, bemoaning, and besmirching."

"The trifecta of B's, huh? I'll take my risks." Blade seemed amused by her description.

"Are you sure? You could wait a few years to see if we're still together," she suggested, giving him an out.

"Who else will be there other than these cousins from hell?" he asked, totally ignoring the escape route she'd offered.

"My parents, my grandmother, my aunt, Ellen, her husband, and Kinsley."

"And the cousins from hell," he added.

"Yes. A ton of family."

"That usually happens at a family barbecue. I'll tell you what. I'll go with you to your barbecue if you come to the clubhouse for dinner next week," Blade proposed.

"Um, that's fine. I already know a lot of the Shadowridge Guardians and their Littles. That would be fun. The shop is closed on Sunday, and my short days are Monday through Wednesday."

"Not a problem. There's dinner at the clubhouse every night. There's also breakfast and lunch. We all take shifts cooking and helping in the kitchen. Gabriel and Bear are usually in charge."

"Oh, I remember meeting them." Sapphire said, grabbing a pepperoni from the last slice.

"Yes, at The Hangout."

The bell tinkled, and a man walked in. Sapphire had seen him before. He'd been hanging around the block lined with small specialty shops for a while—a couple of weeks, at least. He never had packages.

She chewed and swallowed quickly as she stood up. "Hi. Welcome to The Blue Door. What can I help you find today?"

"Just looking."

"Of course. You'll find everything is handcrafted and unique. Rings are at the counter. Necklace and earring sets are on the far wall."

She had a bad feeling about the man and tried to talk herself out of it. People often judged her for her blue hair and tattoos. She didn't want to assume this man was trouble just because he was hanging around and she'd never seen packages. Sapphire definitely didn't run into all the people in the area. She could have missed him on the days he'd purchased something.

"I'll know it when I see it," the customer stated firmly and avoided eye contact.

He picked up and put down a lot of items, making her nervousness increase. *What is it about this guy?*

Suddenly, she noticed him slip a pair of earrings into his pocket. Hell no. That wasn't happening in her store. "Sir, I need you to return the items you placed in your pocket and then leave."

"I don't know what you're talking about," he mumbled and started toward the door.

Sapphire heard the soft grate of Blade's stool on the flooring as he stood. She didn't glance at the biker. She was perfectly capable of dealing with this jerk.

Moving around the shoplifter quickly, Sapphire physically blocked his way to the entrance and stated firmly, "You're on camera. I will call the police. Let me have the jewelry."

Blade's boots resounded on the floor. She heard the snick of something being pulled from leather. The man looked back over his shoulder at Blade, who Sapphire could hear advancing, but she didn't take her eyes off the thief.

"Return that jewelry now," she stated firmly.

He glanced back at Blade one more time and thrust his hand into his pocket. After pulling out the earrings she'd seen him steal and several other items she'd missed completely, the man tossed them onto the countertop. He dodged around her, and Sapphire didn't try to stop him. She did jump in front of the bristling man dressed in leather who rushed toward the door after him.

"Let him go."

Blade stared at her. His brown eyes were narrowed and hard, transforming his face into something scary. Sapphire was amazed that she wasn't frightened.

"Get out of the way, Little girl."

"He's gone, and we're not chasing after him. If he got out of here with anything, it wasn't that big of a deal. I keep the expensive jewelry behind the counter." She didn't look at the large knife in his hand, having already caught a glimpse of it. "Put that away and calm down."

"I don't think you get to tell me what to do," he informed her in an ice-cold voice.

"My store. My rules." She pointed to the camera. "I'd like to call the police and report that man, but they're going to be more concerned about you and that *machete*." Sapphire waved a hand toward the weapon in his hand without glancing at it.

"I don't have a machete hidden in the front of my vest," Blade reassured her. His voice lightened, and his malevolent facial expression eased.

"Thank goodness. Now put it back wherever it goes, please." She looked at the display where he'd spent the most time and noted the holes where products were missing. When her gaze returned to Blade, the knife had disappeared.

"Call the police, Little girl."

"My store. My rules," she reminded him.

"Outside of this store—I have the last word," he told her calmly. "And if you endanger yourself even in your shop, I stop being lenient."

"Lenient?" Her blood started to boil until she saw the clump of jewelry on the counter. What would she have done if Blade hadn't been with her? Within seconds, ice water ran through her veins. She shook with the emotional impact of the confrontation.

Blade stepped forward and wrapped himself around her. "You're okay, Blue Eyes. I've got you."

Sapphire buried her face in the crook of his neck and

wrapped her arms around his waist. His warmth seeped into her frigid body. Slowly she thawed.

"Thank you for being here, Blade."

"Daddy," he corrected her gently.

"Daddy. I should call the police now."

With the assailant gone, no damage done, and no injuries, the police suggested she come to the station when convenient and file a report. Blade was not pleased with that response, but Sapphire understood completely.

"It's Friday night. There are many more serious things the police need to handle. The danger has passed," she reminded him.

"Tomorrow morning, you file a report."

"It will have to wait until Monday or Sunday if I can file a report on the weekend," Sapphire told him as she put the jewelry back on the displays. She made a note to check the display for empty spaces if someone ever came in the store who seemed suspicious. That quick glance could help her keep track of possible shoplifting. Unless she got hit by a stampede of customers, Sapphire tried to fill bare spots with new merchandise immediately.

His look made her explain. "I have Kinsley tomorrow morning. It's the last day my sister will need me."

"She works on a Saturday?" Blade asked.

"She rotates weekends with the other staff at her business. Of course, this is her weekend. Her husband will come pick Kinsley up when he gets in from his business trip that morning. Me taking care of Kinsley at The Blue Door was a necessity caused by a bunch of obligations that all happened just as the regular babysitter had a baby. Next week, everything goes back to normal."

"I don't have to work on Saturdays. I'll come to handle the shop for you and watch Kinsley."

"You don't need to do that. I will let you hold down the fort while I grab some pictures of that guy off my security camera and send a message to the other shops about him," Sapphire requested and backed a step away from him. Blade's arms tightened around her.

"Are you okay now?" Blade asked, studying her face.

Sapphire's shoulders eased back down into place as her stress diminished. He honestly cared about her and would do anything to help. She nodded to reassure him.

"Yeah. I've had to deal with shoplifters before. That guy seemed extra... I don't know what. It bothers me that he's been hanging around the shops in the area. I guess casing the joint. If he was smart, he would have bailed the minute he saw I wasn't alone."

"Who knows what was happening with him? Now, however, you are aware that he's bad news. If you see him, lock the door and call the police. Then call me."

"I can't disturb you. You're working," she said, not wanting him to think he was stuck with someone who needed rescuing all the time. "I've had my shop open for a while. I can handle pretty much anything that comes my way."

"I have no doubt that's true. It will make me feel better if you'll promise to call me for backup—just so I don't worry," he told her gently. "Daddies need to make sure their Littles are safe. Otherwise, we get upset. You don't want me in the hospital with ulcers, right?"

"That's a far jump from needing to protect me to being medically bedridden," she said, unable to keep herself from laughing at the mental image of Blade with knives hidden in his hospital gown.

"I don't want to know what popped into your brain, do I?"

When she shook her head, he continued, "I don't doubt that you can take care of your shop. You are talented and hardworking. I simply want to make sure you're okay. Can you promise to call me if there's a problem?"

"As soon as I can," she agreed.

"Thank you, Sapphire. Now, go grab the photos and send your alerts. I'll try not to scare all your customers away."

Working quickly in the back, Sapphire grabbed screenshots and forwarded them to her phone both as pictures and files she could share. She pulled up her email and messaged the shop-keepers in her area, along with the pictures. She didn't have everyone's contact information but asked the other owners to share the word with others.

The sound of feminine laughter drifted to her from the shop and Sapphire stopped to listen for a moment. Hearing the low tones of Blade's voice, she figured everything was okay. Quickly, she created a concise report for the police that she would drop by the station tomorrow when she had a chance. Having everything put together made her feel better. She wouldn't let that shoplifter get by with hurting small businesses.

Sapphire walked into the shop and froze at the sight of four women practically drooling over the biker behind the counter. He had already packed up three of the orders, and the women held onto bulging bags. Blade grinned her way when he caught sight of her.

"And this is the artist who created the beautiful pieces you're taking home tonight," he shared, waving an arm in Sapphire's direction.

"You are so talented. I love your work," one woman gushed. "Would it be too much to ask that you pose for a picture with us? And then maybe you could take a picture of us with Blade? He's amazing at suggesting jewelry that complements each of us."

There was no doubt in Sapphire's mind that they would delete one picture much quicker than the other. Sapphire looked at Blade to make sure he was okay with that, and when he gave a brief nod, she answered, "Of course. I'm so glad you discov-ered some pieces that you love."

Her eyes widened at the amount on the cash register as she walked forward to join the group. Blade adeptly charged the woman's credit card before placing the boxes into a large shopping bag. With the business complete, they snapped a few photos.

As the women prepared to leave, a brunette asked, "Blade? When do you work in the store? I may need to come back for some gifts."

"I'm afraid I'm not a regular employee. I come in to help Sapphire when inspiration strikes her and she needs some time in the back to create. Feel free to check in often. I might be here," Blade assured them.

"Will do, Blade. Thanks for your help," one called as the women headed reluctantly toward the door.

"What did you do? Juggle knives to impress them?" Sapphire asked in fascination as she looked around the store at all the empty spaces on the racks.

"No juggling necessary. Turns out, I'm good at helping women find pretty things," he said with a grin.

"I think you just sold a month's worth of jewelry in an hour. I should have shoplifters in more often."

"Don't even say that," he warned, sobering instantly.

"You're right. That was in bad taste. It's ten minutes until closing. How about if I clean up quickly and we can get out of here? Would you like to come home with me and visit Silver? He misses you."

"Only if I can spend time with you as well, Blue Eyes."

"I'd like that." Silver would understand that she wanted his attention focused on her. To Sapphire's surprise, she wasn't nervous. She hadn't felt this strongly about anyone before. Being alone with him sounded incredible. Hopefully, she could convince him to stay.

CHAPTER
SIX

Sapphire parked her car, and Blade's large bike backed in next to her. She didn't like thinking that he was preparing to leave even though she had noticed most bikers reversed into a parking space. Turning, she gathered her purse and jacket from the passenger seat and slid out of the car.

She couldn't believe how nervous she felt. It wasn't like she was a virgin or anything. This was important—like being intimate was a big step in their relationship. Lifting her gaze, she met Blade as he stood beside her.

"Come on, Blue Eyes. Show me your apartment. I can't wait to learn more about you," he said quietly.

Staring at him for a full second, Sapphire listened to what that simple message told her. He didn't plan to be a one-night stand. He wanted to see her most private space, because sensing it would give him insights into who she was. "It may be messy. I was in a hurry this morning."

"I already know you're a very organized person. I've seen how you handle your stock at the shop." He held out his hand, and she intertwined her fingers with his. "Let me see the side of you unimportant people don't get to experience."

The pressure seemed to lift from her shoulders. He really

cared about her. She squeezed his hand and nodded before turn-ing. Leading him through the locked building door, Sapphire watched him scan the area and suspected he was checking out the security of the apartment complex. She opened her own door and led the way inside.

Glancing around, she tried to see her apartment like a stranger would. A comfy sectional dominated the space. It had footstools that could either detach or hug the couch. She had the softest blanket thrown over the back of it. It was heaven to snuggle under while she watched movies.

Of course, art filled the walls. As she set her things down on an end table, she watched him walk forward to study a large abstract piece next to the TV. That was one of her most favorite paintings she'd ever created. Full of color and movement, it popped from the wall.

"From my painting era," she joked.

"You are very talented. It reminds me of a waterfall. All the energy in the splashing liquid ricochets everywhere," he shared as he studied it.

"I like that. It's my version of a merry-go-round but sped up. I actually painted it horizontally, but I like it better vertically, so the movement is like a waterfall," she shared, pleased.

He tilted his head one way and then the other. "There it is. I can see that."

"You're just being kind now," she said with a laugh. It died out quickly as he turned to look at her.

"I will never lie to you, Sapphire. That's not who I am. I'll never deliberately be unkind, but I don't like untruths. It's not how I want to live."

Blade walked forward and ran his hands up her arms. "I don't have a silver tongue. I can only tell you what I think or feel. Like, I've never felt this sure about a relationship. You're the one I've searched for."

"I've never had this connection with anyone," she shared.

"Do you want to sit down and talk about it? Or should I pick you up and carry you into the bedroom to make you mine?"

"I can walk," she suggested.

"Not happening." He strode forward and scooped her up into his powerful arms. "Which way?"

"Down the hallway to the right."

He carried her easily into her bedroom and sat her on the jumble of covers that Sapphire had left when she'd bounced out of bed that morning in the rush to get to the shop before her sister. Blade brushed his hand over her hair and leaned in to kiss her softly before scooping up Silver from his lazy spot on one pillow.

"Hello, Silver. I'm glad to see you again. I'm going to put you on the dresser for a bit. There are some things I don't like having an audience for," Blade said, as he walked over to place the teddy bear facing the wall.

Sapphire laughed, delighted at the biker's calm tone as he explained his actions to the stuffie.

Blade returned and stood next to the bed. "We have too many clothes on, Little girl. Let me start and then I'll unwrap my present."

Sapphire stared at him, trying to figure out what he meant. He shrugged out of his leather vest and draped it over a nearby chair. His boots came off next, revealing teddy bear socks. Her gaze flew to his face in shock.

"Not everything I wear has to contain sharp edges," he told her with a smirk.

That humorous grin combined with his chat with Silver made her smile back. She couldn't wait to find out all the special quirks that made him so irresistible. Who knew stuffie socks on a hot biker could be so alluring?

He grabbed a condom from his back pocket and placed it on the nightstand. "I've been tested, Blue Eyes. Is there anything I need to know about your health?"

"I got checked after I broke up with my last boyfriend. I

stopped taking my birth control pills. I've been so busy at the shop...."

"I'll protect you, and we'll make plans for the future later. Are you okay with that?"

She nodded. Thank goodness he had thought of protection. She was so nervous she'd actually forgotten. Totally out of practice.

He didn't hesitate but reached over his shoulder to yank his T-shirt off. She watched the grooves of his abs and chest emerge and couldn't prevent her jaw from dropping. Sapphire had known he was in shape, but... No wonder he had lifted her like she weighed nothing.

Her mind filled with worry. He couldn't be interested in her. She wasn't completely toned, but she hadn't been in the gym since the shop opened.

She glanced up to meet his gaze, ready to make some excuse to save herself from the humiliation of being naked in front of this sculpted hunk. The heat in his eyes made her freeze. He looked at her like she was candy he couldn't wait to devour.

Desire rekindled instantly low in her abdomen. "Blade...."

"Daddy." He interrupted her as he stripped off his belt. The view of the leather strip in his hand made her heart skip a beat.

"Thankfully, you've been a good girl," he growled before throwing it onto the chair.

Sapphire nodded before she realized what she was doing. "That doesn't turn me on," she blurted and her face heated immediately with embarrassment.

"It does, and you'll feel my hand swatting your bottom if you're naughty long before you'd earn a spanking with a belt."

Staring at him, Sapphire struggled to come up with an answer to that statement. How could he know so much about her fantasies? He reached a hand out to lift her chin, gently closing her gaping mouth. Before she could become self-conscious, he threaded his fingers through her hair and deftly removed her scrunchie, letting her tresses tumble around her shoulders.

"You are so beautiful, Blue Eyes."

Blade leaned down to kiss her hard and fast, taking her breath away. She wrapped her arms around his neck to pull him back down, but he circled her waist with his powerful hands and lifted her to stand in front of him. He glided his fingers over her ribcage with an appreciative touch that lingered at the side swell of her breasts and on her hips.

"I feel like a kid who's gotten the best present under the tree. I want to rip off the paper but choose to peel it off perfectly intact to prolong the experience."

The corners of her lips lifted at that relatable emotion. She liked the thought that he considered her a gift. Sapphire held her breath as he glided his hand under the bottom of her shirt. He pulled the hem up slowly as his fingers caressed the flesh they uncovered. Blade paused at her breasts. His thumbs softly rubbed over the lace cups, completely missing her nipples. Suddenly, that was all she could think of.

She craved his touch. Sapphire shifted slightly to guide his touch to where she needed to feel him. He gripped her sides firmly, holding her in place.

"Daddy's in charge, Blue Eyes."

"That's not fair."

"It totally is. My present. My way," Blade informed her with a steely look that told her nothing would change his mind.

She nodded after a slight pause and received another caress over the sides of the lacy bra before he raised her top more. As he pulled it over her head, Blade leaned in to nibble at the sensitive curve of her neck. When he finally tossed the T-shirt to the side, every nerve ending above her waist was on full alert. Waiting for his touch.

Chewing on her bottom lip as she struggled for control, Blade traced the line of her lips with the tip of his index finger. Immediately, she released the pink captive.

"Only I get to bite you now, Sapphire."

She loved the possessive sound of that and the mental picture that popped into her head. A quiet moan escaped from her mouth. His wicked grin made her burn hotter.

He hooked a finger under her bra strap and dragged it slowly down her shoulder before repeating the action on the other side. The soft drag of his rough fingertip over her skin was almost electric. The jolt led straight to her core. Without fumbling or struggling, he popped the front closure of her bra and peeled the cups from her breasts.

Blade pressed a kiss between her breasts and then moved across to one nipple as his fingers unfastened her jeans. So focused on the sensations of his hot mouth wrapping around that tight peak, she couldn't pay attention to anything else. That was, until his hand cupped her bare bottom and squeezed.

At her gasp, he released her nipple with a pop. "This ass is absolutely spankable. Do you know I fight for control over my cock every time you lean over to grab stock from those drawers under the displays?"

Dirty talk? She'd read that in a book once and thought it sounded silly. These growly comments were like gasoline on the fire building inside her. She felt sexier than ever before.

"Make love to me, Blade."

"Wild horses…." He left the rest of that phrase unspoken as he scooped her up in his arms to sit her on the mattress. Blade quickly removed her shoes, socks, and clothing.

She forgot to be nervous as he stepped back to ease the zipper over his erection. Sapphire stared at his thick, long cock with a mixture of blatant ogling and concern. She'd never had a lover so well-endowed.

He thrust his jeans down his thighs and stripped off the rest of his clothing. He had definitely not missed leg day at the gym. Closing the distance between them, Blade stepped forward to stand next to her next to the bed and wrapped arms around her waist. He fell backward onto the mattress, taking her with him.

When the room stopped rotating around her, Sapphire rested on top of his hard chest as they lay sideways across the bed. Her legs had automatically spread to straddle his hips, with her knees pressed against the mattress. She shifted and froze as her pussy slid over his cock. "That's not going to fit," popped out of her mouth.

"It will. Sit up for me, Blue Eyes. I want to look at you."

As she rose, he curled up with her. Blade stroked his hands over her body, cupping and caressing her curves as he tasted her skin. She stroked her hands over his hard shoulders and loved the iron-like strength that lurked just below the surface. Feeling daring, she rubbed her nipples against the scattered hair over his chest, earning a groan from them both.

"You are temptation in a beautiful wrapper, Little girl," Blade told her as he kissed up the cord of her neck to capture her lips.

That scorching kiss made her tighten her fingers to hold on. He explored her mouth, tasting her and tempting her tongue to join his seduction. She loved his flavor and the appreciative sounds that slid from his lips. Blade would not be a quiet lover. Sapphire couldn't wait to hear his pleasure. It was a complete turn-on. A moan filled her throat, and she allowed it to escape.

"Good girl. Always let me enjoy your sounds," he praised her.

He leaned back slightly to run his hands over her back and then up her sides. Cupping her breasts, he rubbed his thumbs over her nipples, giving her that stimulation she'd craved as he undressed her. "Look at these pretty pink nipples. They're the same color as your lips. Do they need kisses?"

"I think you should check."

His slow smile did things to her pulse. "Good idea, Little girl."

He tilted her backward, keeping her safe with an arm wrapped around her waist as he captured one tight peak in his mouth. His tongue traced around it as the heat of his mouth surrounded her. Closing her eyes, she angled her chin upward to concentrate as he sucked strongly. That blend of a tiny bite of pain combined with pleasure made her so wet.

Blade bucked his hips up to press into her wetness. The grind of his thickness against her pussy started promising tingles. Surely, she couldn't come just from this?

Reaching a hand between them, Blade ruffled her neatly-trimmed adult hair. She held her breath. How would he touch her? Taking his time, he traced the edges of her lower lips. Her ample juices quickly coated his fingers. He lifted his fingers to his mouth and licked them.

"Damn, Blue Eyes. You're my new addiction. Taste," he ordered and pulled her forward for a kiss.

In the history of hot moves, that had to compete for the top spot. She clung to him as he shared her flavor. When he lifted his head, she could only stare at him.

"Good, huh?"

She nodded wordlessly.

"I love that you're so wet for me." Blade relaxed down to the mattress and wrapped his hands around her waist. "Sit on my face, Sapphire. I need more."

"Blade, no," she refused, shaking her head.

"Don't tell me no, Little girl, unless that's a hard limit. Do you not like having your pussy devoured?"

"Yes. But… that's embarrassing."

"I'm going to touch every inch of you, Sapphire. Can you be brave for me? Give me two minutes to convince you, and then we'll try something else if you don't enjoy it."

It seemed weird to negotiate in the middle of sex, but at the same time, it was reassuring. He was listening to her and not focusing solely on his own pleasure. "Okay," she whispered.

He helped her move into position and drew her hips down. She shivered at the sensation of his lips and tongue moving so intimately. Blade traced her opening and dipped inside to taste her.

"Mmm." His hum vibrated through her sensitive tissues, drawing an appreciative moan from Sapphire.

She shifted tentatively, unsure what he wanted her to do. Blade rewarded her by circling her clit with his tongue. Sapphire looked down at the erotic scene. His gaze met hers. She couldn't believe the heat contained in his eyes, revealing his desire and enjoyment. Pushing away her self-consciousness, Sapphire concentrated on the sensations he lavished on her. Each different touch brought those swirling tingles closer until they crashed over her.

Her body jerked with the force of her orgasm. Blade did not relent but continued to caress and taste her, extending and deepening the pleasure. She'd never experienced anything so incredible as this.

"Blade, please," she whispered.

"Daddy," he growled against her pussy, making her shiver from the contact.

"Daddy, please. I can't take any more."

"I'm just starting, Blue Eyes." He lifted her easily to shift her back to straddle his hips.

She collapsed on top of him and kissed him hard. Tasting herself on his lips and skin rekindled her arousal. Sapphire rubbed her pelvis on top of his cock. "Your turn, Daddy."

"It's still our turn, Little girl. I'm enjoying our play as much as you are."

He wrapped his arms around her and rolled to reverse their positions. His muscles bulged as he shifted her to rest on the pillows, lengthwise on the bed. "I don't want you to end up sliding off the bed headfirst," he told her with a wink, reminding her of that errant thought that had flashed through her mind earlier.

If anyone could make her stand on her head, it would be this man.

Fascinated by that coincidence as he leaned over to grab the condom, Sapphire understood what differed from other sexual encounters she'd experienced. Blade got her. She loved that he viewed lovemaking on a different level. For him, their pleasure was intertwined. There wasn't one activity that was for her stimulation and another for him.

The sight of his hands moving on his cock fascinated her as he rolled on the condom. Expecting that their play was finished, she waited for Blade to enter her. To her surprise, he lowered his pelvis to her and slid his shaft through her wetness. His path rubbed over several sensitive spots, sending zings of arousal through her.

Exploring his chiseled form with her hands, Sapphire loved finding the places he enjoyed being touched the most as well. His quick inhales and groans were music to her ears. The earthy scent of their heated skin surrounded the couple, and their hands slipped as they caressed each other.

By the time he fitted himself at her entrance, Sapphire had stopped thinking about how she appeared or if she did things correctly. She knew from his sounds and his body's reaction to her touch. Blade entered her slowly, taking his time and allowing her to adjust to his thickness. The faint burn as he stretched her pushed her arousal even higher. When his pelvis met hers, she looked up at him triumphantly. His dark eyes danced with merriment.

"Good job, Little girl," he praised, celebrating her, not like he was laughing at her. She had trusted him, and he made sure he delivered.

"Move, Daddy!" she demanded and then held on as he glided out of her and thrust slowly back in. Could anything feel this good? She wrapped her legs around his waist and joined the sinuous dance.

Gradually, he increased the speed of his thrusts. With a cry, she exploded into another climax. From the sound of his groan, she challenged his control. Sapphire loved knowing he was as into her as she was into him.

Daringly, she traced her fingers down his spine. She cupped his tight ass and ground herself against him, adding more sensations. When he didn't protest, she trailed her fingers between his muscular buttocks to flick lightly over his heavy balls.

"You are playing with fire, Sapphire."

The arousal in his voice thrilled her. "Come, Daddy. I need you to fill me."

Blade slid a hand under her ass and hauled her body up to his. His movement quickened until he plunged into her so deeply she wondered where he stopped and she began. Those telltale tingles heralding her orgasm gathered. She clung to him and met his thrusts with eagerness. With a roar, Blade poured himself into her, triggering her climax as well.

When their heart rates had calmed, Blade rolled to the side to take care of the condom. He gathered her back to his chest and held her close. "Damn, Blue Eyes."

She kissed his chest and squeezed him tight. "That was amazing."

"You're mine, Little girl."

"And you're my Daddy."

He pressed a kiss to her forehead. "For as long as I breathe. Close your eyes. It's past time for Little girls to be asleep."

"You'll stay?" she asked.

"There's nowhere I'd rather be."

CHAPTER
SEVEN

The next morning should have been awkward, but it wasn't. Blade woke her up with a kiss. He even showered with her. Bonus, she'd gotten the shop opened on time.

"What's that?" Her sister pointed to a red mark on Sapphire's jawline. "Looks like stubble burn."

"Just a new overly starched shirt." Sapphire invented an excuse.

"Right. And you just did this?" Her sister pantomimed Sapphire rubbing her jaw awkwardly to hit that spot. Ellen laughed when her daughter tried that move as well.

"See, even Kinsley isn't buying that. So, biker or some other guy?"

"Biker," Sapphire said, appalled that her sister would think she could be interested in anyone while Blade was in her life.

"Hmm. I'm getting increasingly curious about this guy you're seeing. You're safe with him?"

"Give me Kinsley." Sapphire lifted the toddler out of her mother's arms. "He takes better care of me than any man ever has."

"Perfect. I can't wait to meet him." Ellen kissed her daughter and zipped out the door before Kinsley could get upset.

"Want to help Aunt Sapphire with some boxes?" Sapphire bonked a couple of damaged jewelry boxes together, and Kinsley immediately reached for them.

"Mine!"

"They're yours, little girl."

She sat Kinsley in her playpen with the boxes and a few other fun toys. The toddler settled down quickly and had fun with the jewelry boxes. Sapphire had a feeling Kinsley would be artistic like her. The happy child babbled, keeping them both entertained.

The distraction couldn't prevent Sapphire from thinking about the play with Blade in the shower and last night's activities. Dragging her attention back to designing and stocking took repeated determination. Thank goodness the shop was busy. She hadn't daydreamed too much when clients streamed in to browse.

The bells rang at the door, and Sapphire turned to see Remi and Carlee walk in. "Hi!"

"This is your shop? Is that your baby?" Carlee asked.

"My niece, Kinsley. She absolutely loves leather and chews on Blade every time he's here with her."

"Now that's a mental picture," Remi said with a laugh.

"Her real babysitter is off for a few days after having a child," Sapphire shared. "Are you two out shopping today?"

"I remembered the cool earrings you had on, and Carlee thought she'd heard you saying something about this area. We chanced it and came here to explore," Remi explained as she glanced around.

Her gaze focused on one display, and she pointed. "No way. Look at those, Carlee!"

"Aren't those the coolest? Come on. You have to try on some things while you're here," Sapphire suggested.

The next few minutes sped by in a flurry of experimenting

with necklaces and other pieces of jewelry. Dividing her attention as more customers came in, Sapphire flitted back and forth, helping everyone. She loved it when it was busy. Time flew past.

Both Carlee and Remi found some pieces they couldn't live without. They brushed away Sapphire's offer of a discount as she rang them up.

"We want you to stay in business for a very long while," Remi told her.

"I don't suppose you'd show us how to make something simple?" Carlee asked.

"You and Remi?" Sapphire questioned as she boxed up their purchases.

"Well, all the Littles at the MC. I know everyone would be excited," Carlee answered.

"I could do that. Let me brainstorm about it. Would they prefer something for themselves or for the guys?" Sapphire asked.

"Oh, for the guys would be amazing. They'd never expect that," Remi said excitedly. Carlee quickly echoed her decision.

"Okay. I'll put my thinking cap on and experiment a bit. Blade mentioned me coming to dinner at the clubhouse. I'll admit I'm nervous to be around so many new people," Sapphire confessed.

"You're going to love everyone. The guys look fierce, but...," Remi started.

"We promised not to share with anyone that they're really big softies," Carlee finished for her. "Now, you're in on the secret too. You can't tell."

"Oh, I'd never," Sapphire promised. "Do you suppose their women will be okay with me?"

"For sure," Carlee assured her confidently. "Really, you don't have anything to worry about."

"As long as Blade doesn't dump me after meeting my cousins on Sunday," Sapphire told them.

"Blade can handle anyone," Remi said with a grin.

"That sounds dangerous," Sapphire said.

"Blade never comes unarmed. People are always worried about all those weapons. That's not the most dangerous thing about Blade though," Carlee shared.

"We'll expect a full report when we see you at the club-house," Remi said as she picked up her heavy bag of purchases. "Thank you for your beautiful work. I can't wait to show Kade."

"And Atlas," Carlee added.

As the two women headed for the door, Carlee asked, "I'm trying to figure out what to wear first to flaunt these pieces."

"Maybe nothing. That would get Atlas's attention," Remi suggested.

When the door closed, cutting off their giggles, Sapphire hugged herself. She enjoyed them so much. They were like her, only completely different. Now, she couldn't wait to meet the others.

You just have to get through the barbecue.

Sapphire sobered at that reminder. She'd need to take something super delicious to distract everyone. Picking up the phone, she called the bakery just a few doors down and ordered a favorite dessert. Maybe an avalanche of whipped cream would smooth over the digs that her cousins constantly seemed to make.

"Relax, Blue Eyes. It's going to be okay. I promise I won't chew with my mouth open or double dip."

"If they're nasty, we never have to spend time with them again," Sapphire promised.

"What I don't understand is why you see them now if they're this unpleasant?" Blade asked.

"Their mother was my dad's twin. She was the sweetest

woman on the planet. You know, one of those people you can't believe is actually real because they are so good. She passed away in her twenties when my cousins were young. Everyone always excuses all the bad things they say because they lost their mother so early."

"Seems to me your aunt is probably spinning in her grave. They're so awful."

Sapphire wanted to disagree but had to nod. "I don't remember her a lot, but I think you're right. She wouldn't have approved." She met his gaze directly and added, "It's best just to ignore their comments. It's not worth arguing with them."

Blade pulled her close in a comforting hug before leaning back to tell her, "Sweetheart, I don't care what they say about me. I'm a grown-ass man who carves attackers into small pieces. They can't hurt me. What I won't stand for is if they speak negatively about you. I will never allow that."

"It's okay, Blade. I really don't want you to stand up for me."

"It's not okay. And that won't happen. I won't do anything unless they target you. Then, I'll finish it."

"You don't need to do that," Sapphire assured him. "I have thick skin."

"Motorcycle or car?" he asked, changing the subject.

"Motorcycle." She loved feeling the wind over her skin. Getting to the barbecue on the bike might be her only enjoyment during the entire visit. "Oh, but we have the trifle."

"What's a trifle?" he asked, appearing confused.

"It's a layered dessert with cake, fruit, and whipped cream. Completely delicious."

"That does sound good. Show me the dish. If you have a box the right size, we can strap it on the tail of the bike. Or we can take your car," Blade reminded her.

In a few minutes, they'd located a hard-sided cooler where the trifle dish wrapped in a soft towel fit perfectly. With a few small ice packs slid underneath the elevated dish, it would travel safely.

"That works great. It will stay cool while it's out on the table." Sapphire cheered.

"Go put some jeans on under that dress, Little girl. If there's an accident, I don't want you to be unprotected."

"That will look ridiculous, Blade."

"Daddy," he reminded her sternly. "I've seen skin ripped off by the gravel on the road. You're not riding on my bike without coverage. You can shimmy off the jeans when we get there. No one will know."

"Not happening." Sapphire didn't understand why she was choosing this issue to make her stand. Somehow it was important to her that Blade realized he didn't get to order her around.

"Then we take your car."

Sapphire picked up her keys from the kitchen counter, where she always organized them. She dropped them down the front of her dress. "I'm not driving. I'm riding on your bike." When he looked at her with a steely glint in his brown eyes, she squared her shoulders.

Blade checked the clock before stalking forward. "I had hoped to treat you to a ride through the park this morning on the way to your parents' home. Remember, you chose to use that extra time to redo your makeup."

"My makeup?" she said dismissively. Was he blind? "I'm already done with that."

Blade simply leaned over and lifted her over his shoulder. He strolled back to the couch and sat on one of the footrests. In a second, she was stretched over his hard thighs.

"What the h…."

Before she could finish that question, he'd flipped her dress up and pulled her panties down to her knees. Automatically, Sapphire struggled, kicking her legs and trying to roll away from him. Those bulging muscles she'd traced with her tongue last night controlled her attempts with ease.

Whack!

She froze at the stinging swat of his hand on her bottom. It landed again. And again, before she could react. "Stop! You can't spank me!"

"If you're not quiet, your neighbors are going to realize exactly what's happening in here," Blade said softly, as he continued to pepper her tender flesh.

"Stop it, Blade."

"Daddy. You're upset and worried about the barbecue. A reminder of who's in charge will help erase some of that apprehension. You need to trust that I will take care of you."

Struggling to free herself from his powerful hold, Sapphire heard the keys drop out of her dress to the floor. She glared at them. Her bottom felt like it was on fire. He never spanked the same spot twice in a row but spread her punishment over her entire bottom and even down over the tops of her thighs.

The worst thing was the spanking aroused her. It wasn't right to be turned on by his control. She'd always read those spanking scenes in her books with fascination mingled with dread. Sapphire understood now. This was the worst and the best mixed together.

Tears prickled under her eyelids. She tried to blink them away, but the stinging swats kept encouraging her to cry. "Damn it, Blade. Fuck you!"

"We definitely don't have an hour to make love this morning. That 'I've just orgasmed so many times' look on your face won't have a chance to disappear. Unless you want to walk into the barbecue and have everyone know exactly where my cock has enjoyed spending time."

That made her think for a minute. Did she really have a "just screwed" expression? One extra firm spank pushed that distraction from her mind. Unable to process anything other than experience his punishment, Sapphire drooped over his lap as tears tumbled to the carpet.

"Who's in charge, Little girl?"

"Daddy."

"Who's going to keep you safe?"

"Daddy."

Blade rubbed his palm over her bottom. His smoothing hand eased the sting away from her skin and replaced it with a heated burn. "You took your spanking well, Blue Eyes."

She shook her head, denying that statement. Sapphire heard his low chuckle before he scooped her into his arms and cradled her to him. She hissed at the feel of his rough jeans against her hot bottom. "That hurt."

"Yes. You needed something to get your attention."

"I didn't like that," she spat.

"If you promise to be a good girl, I'll change that," Blade said, running his fingers over the slight mound between her thighs.

She froze, anticipating what he'd find. *He can't know!* She'd become wet the moment that first stinging swat had landed. Surely, that wasn't right. Squirming, she tried to free herself.

Just like before, he held her in place easily. "Shh. It's okay, Little girl. I love that you are so responsive. Having your Daddy take control is arousing, isn't it?" He ran his fingers down the crease of her pussy. "Spread your legs, Sapphire. Let Daddy make everything better."

She couldn't refuse him. It was as if he could read her mind. Slowly, she obeyed and moved her thighs apart.

His fingers immediately rewarded her, exploring her pink folds. "So wet, Little girl."

She felt her face warm and knew she was blushing. He kissed her cheek.

"Such an enchanting Little."

Already, he'd memorized ways to please her. Stroking her clit softly before sliding two fingers into her pussy, Blade pushed her arousal higher and higher. He sought that small patch inside her that made her gasp and tapped lightly on it until she squirmed with need.

"Please," fell from her lips.

"Come, Little girl. Soak my hand with your juices," he ordered, squeezing her punished bottom with his free hand.

Seconds later, she climaxed with a loud moan. Her body clamped down on the fingers playing inside her. Zings of pleasure buffeted her until she melted against his chest.

Blade rocked her gently. "Good girl. Do you feel better?"

"Yes. But my butt still stings."

"Reminders from spankings are good. That will help you remember who's in charge," he said wisely. "Ready to go get cleaned up?"

When she nodded, he stood and carried her into the bathroom. "Hold your dress up, Little girl."

Blade wet a washcloth and wiped her juices from her skin. The soft terry cloth rasped across her sensitized flesh. Torn between embarrassment and happiness, she enjoyed his attentions and appreciated the fresh panties he helped her step into.

"Go put on jeans," he reminded her.

She hesitated for a split second, and he smacked her bottom.

"Jeans."

She ran to her closet to find a pair.

CHAPTER EIGHT

"I'll stand right here and shield you, Blue Eyes," Blade said, turning his back after she'd taken off the jacket she'd been required to wear as well.

Sapphire scanned the area. He'd parked next to the bushes that lined her sister's driveway. Between the greenery, his broad form, and the powerful motorcycle, she was about as covered as possible. Quickly, she unfastened her jeans and pulled them off. Her slide sandals were easily dealt with, and within a minute she stood poised and ready to join the party.

"You look edible," he growled, wrapping an arm around her waist.

A flashback to sitting on his face popped into her thoughts. Shocked, she met his gaze. Surely he didn't mean... Oh yes, he did. There was no mistaking the heated arousal in his gaze. "You are bad."

"Very," he agreed. Blade unhooked the cooler, hefting it under one arm, before holding out his free hand. "Introduce me to your relatives."

Shaking her head, Sapphire linked her fingers with his and led him to the backyard. A dozen people stood and sat in groups, chatting. There was a set of long tables, groaning with food. The hubbub of conversation died out as Sapphire called her hello.

A man with salt-and-pepper hair walked forward to greet them. "Sapphire. I'm glad you're here." His gaze landed on their intermingled fingers. "Who's this?"

"Dad, this is Blade Granby."

"I'm glad to meet you, Mr. Jones." Blade slid his fingers from Sapphire's grip and held his hand out. The older man shook it politely.

"Call me Grant. How do you know my daughter, Blade?"

"Dad, this isn't an inquisition. We met at my shop. Blade visited to see if I was interested in doing some designs for him," Sapphire explained. She'd known her parents would treat him politely. They would wonder about his leather cut but would never ask pointed questions or make judgements. They trusted her. They would wonder privately.

"I see," Grant Jones said, scanning Blade from head to toe as a petite woman approached.

"Hi, I'm Bonnie Jones—Sapphire's mother."

"Mrs. Jones. Call me Blade."

"Are those knives sticking out of your vest?" Bonnie asked with astonishment.

"You must be Blade," a cheerful voice interrupted. "I've heard your name babbled a bunch from Kinsley. I'm Ellen. Sapphire's sister."

"I have to ask. How did Sapphire get her name? Ellen, Bonnie, Grant. And then, Sapphire."

"Oh, that was all me. I might have been a bit loopy on drugs, but I'd never seen eyes as blue as hers. I insisted on Sapphire," her mother explained.

"It suits her perfectly." Blade complimented the choice.

"She's just lucky her eyes didn't turn brown a week later," a strident voice announced from behind Sapphire. "That's what happens to some babies born with blue eyes."

The group turned to see a man and woman standing close.

The man added, "She would have had to dye her hair blue or something to live up to that name. Oh, wait. She already did that. And tattooed her skin."

Sapphire rolled her eyes. That duo would have to take the opportunity to make her look ridiculous. Keeping her tone pleasant, Sapphire said, "Blade, let me introduce my cousins, Amelia and Aaron."

"Of course, the cousins." Blade did not reach his hand out to shake theirs. His tone was chilling with an ominous shade of violence—unlike Sapphire had ever heard it.

She shook her head slightly, telling him he didn't need to stand up for her. Sapphire was used to her cousins' belittling statements. They'd been that way all her life.

"And you must be the requisite bad boy boyfriend Sapphire needed to find to fill out her bingo card of weirdness," Aaron added.

"Now, Aaron. Let's ease up on Sapphire," her father gently tried to step in.

"Up. Up. Up."

Everyone looked down at the toddler standing in front of Blade with her arms raised. Kinsley's face was blotchy, as if she didn't feel well. Blade immediately lowered himself to one knee and wrapped his arms around Kinsley when she threw herself against him.

"Blade, I'm sorry. Kinsley is teething and isn't very pleasant to be around. I'll take her and see if I can get her to go settle down with her toys," Ellen suggested as she leaned over to pry the toddler away from him.

"No! Bla!"

"I think she wants to stay with me," Blade said. "We're pretty good friends."

"Watch out, Ellen. Kinsley's been spending too much time with Sapphire. Her aunt's alternative lifestyle choices are starting to wear off on her," Amelia suggested cattily, making Sapphire struggle not to roll her eyes at the jab. "You should have let me babysit instead of going to that ramshackle play-jewelry store."

"Sapphire was an absolute doll to take care of Kinsley, and my daughter loves her aunt," Ellen said stiffly as Blade rose with the toddler in his arms.

Blade patted a sniffling Kinsley on the back and stared directly at one cousin and then the other. "Just to let you know, there's a reason I'm called Blade. I'm very protective of Sapphire and won't allow anyone to speak poorly of her."

"Oh, we were joking. She's used to us kidding around," Aaron said with a chuckle.

"I'm not." Blade's gaze locked with Aaron's until the other man looked away.

"So, you brought your own hitman, Sapphire. What a hoot," Amelia said, appearing completely unsettled despite her bravado.

"She brought the only person who could get Kinsley to sleep. I'm more than grateful to have you here, Blade," Ellen said, waving a hand at the angelic face snoozing on the biker's leather cut. "Besides, all these jokes are old. Surely, we've grown out of picking on each other by now."

"I agree," Bonnie said, beaming at Blade as if he were the mayor of Shadowridge who'd come to join their barbecue.

"Let me get you a beer, Blade," Sapphire's father volunteered.

"Thank you, Grant, but I'll take a soft drink. I don't drink when Sapphire is riding on my bike," Blade answered.

"You're a good man, Blade. I like you already," Grant complimented him. "Ellen makes the best lemonade. Can I get you a glass?"

"I'd like that. Thank you."

"Blade, come say hello to my husband, Stan. He's minding the grill, but he's always wanted to ride a motorcycle. Beware. He will have lots of questions," Ellen said, looping her arm with Blade's.

"You okay, Blue Eyes?" Blade asked.

"I'm good. Go talk to Stan," Sapphire encouraged. Her brother-in-law would be tickled to meet anyone who could save him from his daughter's tears. Kinsley had her daddy wrapped around her little finger.

Daddy. Oh, how that word could mean such different things.

"Sapphire, come talk to me. I haven't heard what you're doing in your shop these days. And you'll have to tell me how you and Blade met," her mother said, linking her arm with Sapphire's.

"That's got to be a good story. Sapphire was standing on a corner...," Aaron started and closed his mouth with an audible snap when Sapphire's mother whirled around to shake a finger at him.

"Aaron Jones. You may either talk nicely to Sapphire or leave. I may be old, but I understand what you are insinuating, and I'm appalled at your manners. Or lack of them. That's the last time I want to hear you say something mean-spirited to Sapphire. Or to Blade. Ellen only invites you and your sister because I insist."

Sapphire's mouth fell open as she replayed her mother's words in her mind. Her mother was an absolute angel, but she always tried to make everyone happy. Sapphire couldn't believe her mom had said any of that.

"Yes, Aunt Bonnie. I'm sorry. I was teasing," Aaron apologized stiffly.

"That teasing stops today. You're not good at it. Unless you're deliberately trying to be mean," Bonnie told him as Sapphire looked on in shock.

"Of course he isn't. Aaron, enough with the bad comedian routine." Amelia turned on him.

"You too, Amelia. Be nice or leave," Bonnie told her. "Come on, Sapphire. Let's sit in the shade. I want to catch up."

Sapphire glanced back over her shoulder as the cousins looked at each other. What had just happened here? It was as if Blade's stance had shown her family how wounding her cousins tried to be. The corners of her mouth tilted upward. The Shadowridge Guardians MC cared for their own. Who knew she'd just needed a biker group in her corner?

"Thanks, Mom," Sapphire said, sitting in a chair. It took effort not to wince at the effect of the hard Adirondack chair on her punished bottom.

"I don't understand them. And I'm sorry. I should have said something long ago. Tell me about Blade. He's different from the other men you've dated."

"He's definitely unique. Blade came to the shop to talk to me about designing a stone embellishment for weapons he crafts for motorcycles. He'd seen a bolo that I'd made for a cowboy."

"Now, what's a bolo?" her mom asked.

Sapphire smiled and explained. They were immersed in a conversation when Ellen came to join them with three glasses of lemonade.

"Oh, I lost track of time. Do you need some help?" her mother asked.

"Nope. With Blade as the baby whisperer, I got everything ready in a jiffy. It's amazing what you can get finished without a toddler clinging to your leg."

"She's such a good girl," Bonnie praised. "I love watching her learn new things."

"She is. Sapphire showed her how to draw on paper. Now she loves decorating everything. My hallway became an art gallery last week," Ellen shared.

"Make sure to use that special tape on paint," Bonnie urged.

"Oh, no. I mean, the actual walls are an art gallery."

Sapphire tried not to laugh. "She got quiet for a few minutes, huh?"

"Exactly. When I found her, my makeup was almost depleted. Do you know how hard it is to get lipstick off a wall?" Ellen asked.

"Scrape off and then use white toothpaste," Bonnie counseled. When both her daughters turned to stare at her, she added, "Sapphire lured you into joining her decorating efforts a lot until I learned to put my makeup on the top shelf."

The women laughed together, drawing the attention of the cousins who had been talking a few feet away. This time when Amelia and Aaron joined them, they were much better mannered. Sapphire actually enjoyed the gathering.

When they got ready to leave, Blade sent Sapphire to the bathroom with her jeans. She returned a few minutes later to find him chatting with her parents. "Here, Blue Eyes," Blade said, holding her jacket out for her to slip into.

"Don't you get hot in that?" her father asked.

"It's better she's protected in case something happens. Once we're on the road, the breeze makes it comfortable," Blade answered easily.

"Oh, I hadn't thought of that. You see kids on bikes all over in T-shirts and shorts. Even flip-flops," Bonnie said.

"That's before they have their first accident. Skin grafts are not pleasant," Blade pointed out.

"I'm glad you're taking care of Sapphire," Grant said, quietly.

"She's important to me. I'll always do my best to keep her safe and happy," Blade answered before Sapphire could think of something to say.

"Thank you for joining us, Blade." Bonnie stepped forward and gave him a hug.

Her dad shook his hand and patted him on the shoulder. "We'll look forward to seeing you next time."

Happiness flooded Sapphire's brain. She'd worried about bringing Blade and he'd fit into her family with ease—by being himself. She shook her head mentally and vowed to trust Blade in new situations.

Her parents stepped back as Blade put on his helmet and fastened Sapphire's into place for her. She waited for him to throw his leg over the bike and lift it into position. When she moved to settle behind him, Blade balanced the bike between his powerful thighs and pulled her close. He zipped up the front of the jacket before telling her, "Now you're ready, Blue Eyes."

Sapphire slid onto the seat and wrapped her arms around his waist. Amelia opened her mouth, and snapped her jaw closed when Aaron elbowed her. What an amazing difference! Sapphire knew it wouldn't last. They'd soon fall back to their crappy ways, but for today, she'd take this as a win.

CHAPTER
NINE

B lade slid the last tub of supplies into his closet. Leaving half-completed projects, tools, and his own cache of weapons out around his rooms was okay when he was alone. Sapphire was going to spend the night at the clubhouse tonight after dinner. He didn't want her to feel like she lived in a battle zone or to hurt herself on one of the fine edges he prided himself on creating.

Scanning the room, he thought it looked bleak. *Crap!*

He whipped open the door, planning to go check in the supply area if there were any decorations or knickknacks to make the place homier.

"Whoa," Steele said, tucking Ivy behind him. "You're in a rush."

"Sorry. I was headed for the storage area."

"What happened to all the stuff?" Ivy asked as she peeked into his room.

"I've figured out my decorations are things Little girls could get hurt playing with," Blade admitted.

"I hope you find what you're searching for," Steele said, tugging Ivy down the hall.

"Wait, Daddy. This place needs a lot of work. It's scary in

there," Ivy declared dramatically. "All empty spaces and shadows. I bet it echoes."

She paused before calling, "Hello?" into the room.

Blade listened for a response before catching himself. "That's silly, Ivy. It's not that bad."

The Little girl shook her head to refute that statement.

"Blade! There's a guy in the shop who wants to talk to you about decking out his vintage hog," Kade called down the hall.

"Ivy, I need some help. Would you mind asking a few of the other Littles to spruce up my apartment so I won't frighten Sapphire?" Blade asked. "Don't lift anything heavy or climb ladders. No paint. Just throw a few pillows around."

"I've got you, Blade. I want an exchange," Ivy said quickly.

"What's that?" he asked suspiciously.

"Can you make me something I can wear that I can use as self-defense? Like a necklace or a bracelet? I still get scared leaving the bank at night," Ivy confessed.

"You should have told me," Steele growled from behind her.

"No way. You'd have camped out in the parking lot in a makeshift welding shop to make sure you had me in your sights at all times. I'm not in danger. The problem is here," Ivy explained, tapping her brain. "Not out there."

"That sounds like something Sapphire and I need to collaborate on. I'll do my best, Ivy," Blade assured her.

"Thank you. Leave your decorations to us," Ivy said, beaming at him.

"Nothing too over-the-top, right?" Blade asked.

"Gotcha," Ivy promised.

"Blade? Are you coming?" Kade bellowed.

Blade turned and jogged down the hall as he answered, "Tell him to keep his chaps on. I'm on my way."

"Come get me when you need the ladder," Steele told Ivy.

"No ladders," Blade reminded them.

"Hi, Blue Eyes," Blade said, looking up to see Sapphire hovering quietly just outside his work area.

"Hi. I didn't want to interrupt you and cause you to get cut," she said as she walked forward.

"That's very thoughtful of you. I'm pretty steady. These guys aren't quiet. I'm used to people stopping by to say something," Blade assured her as he set the adapted handlebar on his workbench. Standing, he pulled her close for a hug before kissing her deeply.

"Mmm. You taste good," Blade complimented. "I've missed you today."

"I missed you too."

"Did you bring your things?"

"I didn't want to walk through the shop like a harlot moving in," she said, turning slightly pink.

"First, no one says harlot anymore. Second, no one here would ever think to judge you like that. Third, let's drive your car around to the clubhouse, and I'll carry your bag to my room. Then, I'll be the harlot," he teased.

"You!" she protested, smacking his chest.

"Come on, Blue Eyes. Let's get you settled."

Taking her hand, he led her through the shop. He liked that several people remembered her name and greeted her personally. When she came to dinner at the clubhouse, he would make it official that she was his.

"Want me to drive?" he asked.

"Please. I don't want to run over a motorcycle or someone. Is it always so busy here?" Sapphire asked, leading him to the last parking spot where she'd left her car.

"Business is good. Between all the guys' talents and the

explosion of popularity of riding, the shop is almost too busy. They could use two of me."

"No one would want to go to the other guy," Sapphire said confidently.

"Talk like that gets you an extra dessert tonight," Blade told her with a wink.

"I like dessert. Chocolate is my favorite."

"I wasn't suggesting something to eat, Little girl," he corrected her, opening the passenger door.

"A dessert that's not something to eat?" she asked in confusion as she sat down.

"Think sexual favor," he suggested and closed the door as she caught on to what he was implying.

"You are so bad," she told him when he got in behind the wheel.

"Bad is the new good, Little girl."

"Are you sure everyone is going to be okay with me staying at the clubhouse?"

"Yes. There are a lot of couples there. And other Littles."

"Oh."

"Next time when you come in, take this road around the shop, and you can park at the clubhouse," he said as he drove that path.

After parking, he squeezed her thigh lightly. "Stay here. I will help you out."

When she nodded, he circled the car to open the door. "Good girl," he praised her as he held out a hand.

"My bag is in the trunk."

With her duffel in one hand, Blade wrapped his other arm around her waist and guided her into the clubhouse. Gabriel waved from the kitchen area where he was working on dinner and called, "Welcome, Sapphire. I hope you're hungry."

"Starving," she answered before adding, "It smells delicious in here."

"Gabriel takes care of us," Blade told her before asking the man cooking, "Where is everyone?"

"You're going to see them soon," Gabriel answered without giving any details.

Blade looked at Sapphire and shrugged. "Come on, sweetheart. We'll stash your bag, I'll give you a tour, and we'll eat."

She followed him past the bar and pool tables to the door that led to their private apartments. The quiet of the almost-empty gathering room morphed into a tumble of giggles and deep chuckles.

What is going on?

"It sounds like a party," Sapphire commented.

"Let's go find out." Blade led the way down the hall and turned the corner. There he stopped in his tracks. Blue shimmering beads hung in the open doorway. Was that a flash of a feathered boa?

Blade pulled some of the lines of sparkling beads aside and ushered Sapphire into his previously boring apartment. They both studied the room. *Welcome, Sapphir* was written on the wall using adhesive hooks, and the final E was underway as Ivy, Elizabeth, and Remi guided a blue string of fluff into place.

Everywhere he looked, the Littles had left their mark. The refrigerator was gift-wrapped with blue paper and a giant bow. A blue scarf draped over the lamp by the couch gave the room an underwater glow. A large sapphire dish sat in the middle of the coffee table, filled with candy.

"Wow!" Sapphire said with her hands clasped to her chest.

"Welcome, Sapphire!" resounded around the room.

"Ivy, you have certainly added some homey touches," Blade said, choosing his words carefully as he controlled the grin that threatened to curve his lips. Only Littles would consider this the equivalent to scattering a few pillows around. Sapphire's reaction made it all perfect.

"Do you like it, Sapphire? Blade was afraid it was too blah in here and asked if we'd make it more fun," Ivy said, bouncing off the couch to stand in front of Sapphire.

"It's absolutely gorgeous. Thank you, Ivy," Sapphire said and gave the woman a quick hug.

"You're welcome. We were rushed, or we could have done more," Ivy told her.

"Wait until you see the bedroom," Remi teased.

"Sapphire needs some time to settle into her azure palace before we eat. Thank you, everyone," Blade announced and shooed everyone out the door. As he closed it, Blade was tickled to see the beads stayed outside.

"You wanted to spruce up the place?" she teased.

"It was very dull. I suggested a few throw pillows on the couch," Blade explained, looking around. Not over-the-top certainly had a different meaning to a bunch of Little girls. Sapphire hadn't stopped smiling. He mentally thanked Ivy, Elizabeth, and Remi for easing Sapphire's apprehension at staying with him.

"Are you angry at them?"

"Not at all. We can take down anything you don't like."

"I love it all, but maybe we could put Blade up there too?" she asked, pointing at her name in feather boas.

"Let's hang a knife with our combined work on it. The first piece can go here," he suggested.

"A blade for Blade. That's so fun. And it will be ours."

Tears gathered in her eyes, and he pulled her close. "I'm so glad your talent and my sharp edges are bringing us together. We have to keep the first one as a souvenir. It's going to be a battle to let the pieces go, but your artistry will be showcased all over the world."

Blade kissed her tenderly. Planning to never let her go, Blade looked forward to their future plans together. It seemed to be an indication that they were supposed to be together.

"Show me the rest of your place."

"I'm hoping you will think of it as our place soon, but let's go check out what they've done." Stepping away, Blade grabbed her bag and took her hand. He led her into the bedroom. There, he stopped to take in the new decorations as Sapphire glanced around for the first time.

"They put in a naughty corner and a toy chest?" she asked in disbelief, seeing the chair facing the corner with a paddle hanging on the wall near it and on the opposite side of the room, the large wooden chest that brimmed with games, puzzles, and toys.

"No, I had already placed those there. I've gathered a few things over the years in the hope that I'd find you, Blue Eyes."

"What did they add here, then?" she asked. Her face was a picture of confusion.

"See the blue ribbon around the paddle and the blue fluffy blanket on the back of the chair? There's a nightlight on your side of the bed now and a sippy cup on the nightstand," Blade pointed out.

"That's it? I was expecting a lot more based on the other room. Don't get me wrong, I love everything, but I'm debating whether I can appear in the main area if everyone has already figured out I'm Little. They're going to look at me differently," Sapphire stated with a waver in her voice.

"Do you think of the other women differently now that you've learned more about them?" Blade asked gently. He understood it was scary that a secret she'd hidden for so long was out there.

"No. I like them all."

"Have they seemed judgmental? Or mean-hearted?"

"No. They've been super sweet," Sapphire admitted.

"Do you care if they drink from cups with a lid and a spout?"

"No, of course not!" She looked offended at that suggestion.

"If they know you're one of them and they want to welcome you, is that bad?" Blade probed. He walked forward and pulled the blanket off the chair. Returning to her side, he wrapped her in the soft fabric and lifted her into his arms. Blade took a seat on the side of the bed, with Sapphire cuddled on his lap. He rocked her softly back and forth, giving her time to process everything.

"This is so nice," Sapphire whispered, rubbing her face against the velvety material. She tilted her head a bit to make eye contact and added, "You're not too shabby either."

Blade's heart lurched in his chest at the adorable picture of her staring up at him with those beautiful eyes. He filed that mental image away to remember forever. "I'm so glad I found you, Little girl. I promise. This is a safe place for you."

"And if it isn't?"

"Then that jackass will be gone. But anyone who would hurt a Little was eliminated long ago from the Shadowridge Guardians MC. They don't exist in the club now. Left are my brothers who would lay down their lives for me or you," Blade told her.

"Why me? Some haven't even talked to me."

"You're mine. We protect what's ours," Blade shared.

His definite tone must have resonated inside her. He watched a stunning smile spread across her lips. Sapphire wiggled her arms out of the cover and wrapped them around his neck to pull his mouth to hers. She kissed him enthusiastically before leaning back.

"Then I'm going to stop worrying. I'll enjoy my time here, being myself. I think I'm going to like it here," Sapphire declared.

"That's my good girl." Blade rewarded her with a kiss before asking, "Want to go get some dinner?" Sapphire often missed meals if her store was too busy for her to stop and eat.

A loud growling sound came from under the blue cloth. Sapphire slapped her hand over her tummy. "I think my body answered for me."

"Let's go." Blade boosted her to her feet and stood.

"Can I let Silver out of the duffel first? I don't want him to get squished."

"You can take him to dinner if you wish," Blade told her as

he grabbed her case from the floor just inside the doorway and plopped it on the bed.

"Take him to dinner?" Sapphire echoed. "Oh! They won't look at me strangely here. I think Silver is hungry."

"Then he needs some food. Let's see if Gabriel can tempt him," Blade suggested.

Sapphire quickly unzipped her bag and extracted the fluffy teddy bear. She hugged Silver to her chest and announced, "We're ready."

Blade held out a hand for hers and led her out of the door, through the dangling beads that reappeared when it was open. "Those are going to have to go away," he grumbled.

"Could we leave them for a while, so I'll remember which room is yours?"

"Only for you, Little girl. And because I'll keep you with me as often as you'll stay," Blade told her. "Permanently would be ideal for me."

"You don't want me here every day," she said, walking sideways down the hallway to watch his face.

"I'll move you in tomorrow if you say so. I'm not planning to sleep alone again."

"Oh. I like snuggling with you, too. Could we alternate between my apartment and the clubhouse for a while?" she asked.

"Of course. We can decide to live either place. As long as we're together, Blue Eyes, I'm happy."

"Sapphire, Sapphire, Sapphire." The chanting of her name started the minute they appeared in the gathering room.

"I'm going to guess they're glad you're here, Little girl," Blade told her as he rubbed her back reassuringly.

"Dinner is served," Gabriel called, shifting everyone's attention away from Sapphire.

Blade felt her relax and sent his MC brother a nod of appreciation. "Let's get in line. How about if I pile one plate with food and we can both try everything?"

"Things can't touch," she said in horror at that idea.

He hadn't noticed that she preferred to have her dish with each item separate. He'd have to think about the past meals they'd had together to see why he hadn't picked up on that. For now, he had an easy solution.

"Gabriel, could I have one of the special plates? A blue one if you have it."

"Coming right up," Gabriel opened a cabinet under the long counter where the food was displayed and stood up with a bright blue plate that was molded to have different compartments.

"Me too, Gabriel?" Ivy asked behind her. "I don't like it when my potatoes get fruit juice on them."

"How about a green one to match your eyes?" Gabriel suggested.

"Thank you. That's perfect!" Ivy declared.

Blade offered Sapphire a roll with the tongs, and she pointed to one of the spaces. As they progressed down the display of food, he helped her with some things, and she wanted to serve herself with others. By the time they got close to the end, he noticed she had passed on all the green options. The last dish was a tempting platter of raw vegetables and dip.

"You need some veggies, Sapphire. Do you like baby carrots?" he offered her.

"Too orange," she answered.

"Celery?"

"Too green."

"Peppers?"

Sapphire sighed and said, "Only the red ones."

He put three slices on her plate and pointed at the broccoli.

"Too fuzzy. I'll take a piece of cauliflower. But just one," she said quickly.

"Do you want dip?"

"I don't have a place for it," she refused.

As if by magic, a small shot glass appeared on her tray. Blade winked at Gabriel. That guy was a pro.

"That will work. Can you put some in for me, Daddy?" Sapphire asked and gasped. She looked around to see if anyone had caught what she'd said. Blade winked at her as he celebrated inside. He was beyond happy that she thought of him as her Daddy.

"Daddy, can I have a container for dip too?" Ivy asked Steele.

"Of course. Gabriel? Another shot glass, please?" Steele called to the man in the kitchen.

"I should put out a bunch of those," Gabriel suggested and produced a half dozen.

Blade carried his plate and her tray to a big empty table. "I'm going to get us some drinks, Sapphire. Don't let anyone steal my seat," he warned playfully. When Sapphire waved a hand, urging him closer, he leaned down to talk to her privately.

"They didn't say anything about me calling you Daddy," she whispered urgently.

"And they never will. This is a safe place, Little girl."

Ivy appeared and said, "Your Daddy's there, right?"

When Sapphire nodded, Ivy said, "Can I sit next to you on this side and then my Daddy can take that chair there?"

"I'd love that," Sapphire answered.

As Blade walked away with Steele to get their drinks, Ivy asked what Sapphire's teddy's name was. The two were chattering happily as the guys walked out of hearing range.

"That Little girl of yours is going to settle in perfectly," Steele observed, whacking Blade on the shoulder companionably.

"Perfect is exactly what she is."

CHAPTER
TEN

is Little girl disappeared into the blanket fort Kade and Faust had created for the Littles after dinner without a hint of hesitation. The giggles that ensued shortly after made him happier than Blade had been for many years. Sapphire had run back to dash through the beads to grab some elastic string and beads. It appeared that the Littles loved making bracelets.

After helping Gabriel clean the kitchen, Blade challenged Storm to a rematch at darts. "Come on, you can help me keep my targeting honed."

"You're a fucking beast throwing anything with a point," Storm groused.

"Maybe you'll win this time," Blade suggested.

"Not a chance in hell, but I'll see how close I can get," Storm told him.

"I could play left-handed?"

"Fuck you. Like I want these guys to see you beat me that way too." Storm looked at the bar. "Grab me a beer. I'm going to need fortification."

After a fierce battle that drew onlookers, Blade shook Storm's hand. "Thanks, brother. You're a worthy opponent. Let me know if you want to try the left-hand thing for the next game."

"Cocky bastard," Storm growled good-naturedly. He realized he'd played well against the unequaled champion. "Buy me a drink."

"You got it."

"Daddy? Can we have some juice?" Brooke asked.

"That's a lot of sugar before bed, Little girl. How about some water or milk?" Storm asked, ruffling her adorable curls.

"Chocolate milk?" Brooke asked, giving him a winning smile.

"You got it," Storm agreed, holding out his hand for hers.

A flurry of activity at the entrance to the blanket fort drew the men's attention. "She got it," Carlee's voice sounded inside. A cheer resounded under the muffling covers.

Blade shook his head, sure that the group had targeted the chocolaty beverage from the beginning. The Littles made their lives interesting.

Blade couldn't keep the smile from his face the next morning. Last night had been an enormous success. Waking up this morning with Sapphire cuddled to his chest had started the day off with a bang. With Kinsley now back at her sitter's, his Little's need to get to the shop early had evaporated. Their lovemaking had put them both in an excellent mood.

Blade assembled a package of unsharpened weaponry that needed Sapphire's jeweled embellishments. He'd make a trip to The Blue Door to see her. Finding Kade in the shop's office, he leaned against the door.

"Hey. I'm taking a bunch of hilts to Sapphire for her to jewel. I'll be back in a couple of hours," he said to Kade.

"Don't forget you have that appointment for a consultation at three," Kade reminded him, pointing at the calendar on his wall.

"I'll be back," Blade assured him.

"Is she going to be here tonight?" Kade asked. "Remi likes her."

"She's pretty incredible. Yeah. They're doing nails this evening. Sapphire's promised to bling out their manicures."

Kade rolled his eyes. "Get ready. We're going to have a bunch of fingernails to ooh and ah over."

"And you'll love every minute," Blade predicted.

"Damn, Blade. Would you carry your phone with you? It's been going off every few seconds," Faust complained.

Blade grabbed the device, noticing five missed calls from Sapphire. As if on cue, the ringer blared loudly. Quickly, he answered it. "Sapphire? What's wrong?"

"He's back. I locked the doors and called the cops, but he's banging on the windows. I think he's going to break in."

"I'm on my way." Blade held the phone to his rapidly thudding heart and said, "Anyone want to scare a thug straight?"

In seconds, a posse of Shadowridge Guardians were on the road to The Blue Door. Blade had switched the phone call to the headset wired into his helmet to continue talking to Sapphire. "Three minutes and I'll be there. Where is he now?"

"He disappeared from the front. Wait. The security camera just picked him up at the back entrance."

"Is it locked, Little girl?" He tried to keep his voice calm as he increased his speed. His gut twisted inside as he rushed to her side. The downtown traffic and lights limited his progress, increasing his frustration and worry.

"Yes. Always. Hurry, Blade. He's banging on the door with something. Where are the police?"

"I'm coming, Blue Eyes. Go lock yourself in the bathroom," he ordered as he raised one arm to point to the right. Steele and Faust peeled off from the group, understanding completely

Blade's request to split into the alternative route. He'd come in through the rear parking lot.

Finally, he turned into the industrial space behind the building where deliveries happened and the employees parked. Racing to The Blue Door's back entrance, he saw the man trying to batter his way inside. He'd never parked his bike faster in his life. Jumping from the seat, he ran forward.

"Hey! Why don't you pick on someone your own size?" he bellowed to distract the thug. In the distance, sirens blared, growing in volume. He'd have to work quickly to deal with this before the police arrived. The Shadowridge Guardians' way of dealing with anyone who threatened one of theirs was much harsher than the authorities would be.

The man whirled with a tire iron hoisted above his head. Blade didn't hesitate. He threw a knife from his vest toward the man's hand holding the weapon as he swung. The blade pierced his wrist, and the metal rod clattered to the ground. Without reacting to the pain, the assailant wheeled around and snatched the tire iron in his other hand. He retreated to the left of the battered door.

Blade saw the Shadowridge Guardians move into place to back him up. "You're not going to win this," Blade admonished him as he readied another knife. This wouldn't end well. One of the guys would have already started videotaping to prove Blade's restraint.

Glaring at him, the man stood silent. Not moving. Not talking. Five feet separated him from the MC.

"Blade? Is it over?"

Sapphire's voice attracted everyone's attention. The man moved unbelievably fast to grab Sapphire's arm and pull her out of the doorway. He held her in front of him like a shield, making Blade's blood boil. His wild eyes focused on Blade. He gripped Sapphire's arm in his injured hand. The injury weakened him, but whatever fueled the aggressor also allowed him to ignore the pain.

Readying the knife he'd pulled the moment the last one had left his grip, Blade yelled, "It's over. Stop."

A police car squealed to a halt, and an officer leapt into action. He shouted, "Drop your weapons" before calling for backup.

Blade nodded, unwilling to take his eyes off Sapphire. The MC members reluctantly eased back. "He's got my girl. I'm not putting away my knife until she's free."

"Drop it," the cop bellowed, dismissing Blade's reasoning.

"Ow! You're going to break my arm. Let me go!" Sapphire protested loudly.

"Sir, release the woman. Hurting her will not help you," the police officer yelled to the assailant.

Sapphire's yelp of pain ended Blade's self-control. He launched the knife in his hand, hitting the man square in his left shoulder. The brute's arm dropped like a rock, and the metal clattered as it struck the pavement. Sapphire twisted out of his hold and ran for Blade. He hugged her and placed her behind him, already rearmed.

The police officer walked closer to the two men. "Someone tell me what's going on here."

"He's been lurking around. He tried to shoplift a bunch of things from my shop. Blade warned him never to come back. This time he's violent. Look at my door," Sapphire told him. Her voice was high and shaky.

Blade suspected she was on the edge of tears. "Wrap your arms around me, sweetheart. I need you to hug me."

Instantly, she encircled his chest with her hands, plastering herself to his spine. The man lurched from his position against the wall. He took one step forward and fell to the ground, twitching from the Taser deployed by the officer. Blade restored his knife he still held to its normal spot as he backed away from the now-prone man. He had extras to replace the one still lodged in the assailant's wrist. The police would keep that one as evidence.

Three more squad cars raced into the parking area and officers rushed to help.

"You waited to let that officer overpower him," Sapphire whispered into his ear.

"You don't need to see me take him down. Are you okay?" he asked, turning around after seeing the perp handcuffed. Unwilling to rely only on his sight, Blade ran his hands over her. Other than blood from her attacker on her clothing and her understandable fright, Blade decided she was unharmed.

"Sir, I'm afraid you'll have to come downtown too. That's standard protocol for any disturbance where weapons are involved," the officer said.

"Of course, officer. My brothers will send the video of the incident to the captain, and my lawyer will meet me there," Blade said calmly. "You'll want to give me some time to remove my weaponry before you search me."

"Blade!" A new arrival dressed in a suit called as he approached. Blade smiled at the familiar man.

"Hi, Detective Newel. How's that bike?"

"Don't tell my kids, but it's the prettiest thing under my roof. After my wife, of course," the detective said with a laugh as he reached out a hand to shake Blade's.

The detective looked at the other officer and said, "You don't have to take him in. We know where to find him. Besides, those are all wounds to impair. If Blade had wanted to kill him, he would have been gone with the first edge that hit him. Get the suspect to the hospital to be patched up. Keep him under guard with the leg shackles on the entire time."

"Blade, introduce me to this lady you're protecting and then walk away for a few minutes while I get her story," the detective requested.

Every hell-no fiber of defiance stood on end inside Blade. He realized he was bristling when Sapphire stroked his chest, trying to calm him. Blade also didn't care.

"I've got this, Blade. He's doing this to wrap up the facts

about that guy. To protect both of us. Go check on your bike," Sapphire told him softly.

Blade studied her face. He didn't like the strain and fatigue etched into her features. His first thought was to wrap her up and steal her away from this situation. The second was how hard she would fight against that. Sapphire was right. This had to be taken care of, and while he could support her, Blade had to allow her to get through this process.

He glared a warning toward the detective. "Be nice."

"Gotcha. I will ask tough questions, but I understand she's not the criminal," the detective assured him.

"Thanks." Turning his attention to Sapphire, he said, "I'm right over there. Make a peep and I'm at your side."

At her nod, he turned and paced away. Each step felt like a mistake. When he reached the clump of MC brothers, Blade forced himself to focus on them even as he monitored the interview behind him.

"Thank you for backing me up," Blade said, as he tried to shake the tension out of his shoulders and jaw.

"We're like the old slogan, 'All for one and one for all,'" Breaker answered.

"I'm no fucking musketeer," Faust growled. Molly had softened the antagonistic MC member's rough edges a lot, but Faust was always antagonistic. The Guardians accepted him the way he was.

"That knife through the wrist in motion was a skilled throw, Blade. Remind me never to piss you off," Ink told him.

"Storm's never going to beat you, is he?" Kade asked.

Blade shook his head. He understood they were trying to distract him. Movement caught his eye, and he turned without saying a word to meet Sapphire halfway.

"All done?" he asked, wrapping his arms around her. He could feel her still trembling, but not as severely as before.

"Yes. He was nice. It was a lot to go over again. I keep seeing that guy reach out to grab me in my brain. It's as scary now as it was then," she admitted.

"I'm sorry, Blue Eyes. That shouldn't have happened to you."

"The detective said by the time they get him seen at the hospital and processed at the station, he'll be there for a couple of days at least. He thought there might be some mental health issues that needed to be addressed."

"Might be?" Blade repeated, feeling his anger rebuild.

"Shh," she soothed him. "There's nothing we can do about their process. You already have a connection with that detective. They don't usually show up for something like this. He heard the responding officer's report that the Shadowridge Guardians were here on the scene of a hostage situation and sped here to help."

The tension faded from his body. "He was great to work with. He's seen a lot."

"Thank you," she whispered.

"You don't need to thank me," Blade said in surprise.

"I do. And all the guys. Take me over there so I can tell them as well."

"Come on, Little girl. Let them know you're okay."

CHAPTER
ELEVEN

apphire glued herself to the powerful shelter Blade's hard form provided. Without asking, he handled everything. Men already bustled around replacing the back door and upgrading its level of protection. When they finished, a new camera system would allow a wide view of everything in the front and rear of the building, as well as inside.

The neighboring business owners alerted by the police canvassing the area stopped by to express their concern and support. One even offered her daughter, who was home from college, as a person to run the shop for her to take the day off. Sapphire had thanked the woman but refused, knowing the daughter would be lost in the shop without training.

"I need to find someone to work with me," she admitted when they were alone inside The Blue Door.

"Can you afford it?" Blade asked.

"Yes."

"Would having someone else here part-time or full-time free you up to design and create new pieces?"

"Definitely." Sapphire's mind boggled at the idea of not having to stop to wait on customers as she devised new creations.

"Do you think it's possible to find an employee who loves your jewelry and would connect with the shop visitors?"

"Of course," she answered, slightly offended at his question. He liked her designs, didn't he?

Blade simply raised an eyebrow at her tone and expression as he seemed to read her mind. "You already know I think you're extraordinarily talented. Back to the quandary about help. It sounds like you've already got a profile of who you need. Let's get a sign in the window."

It took her longer to design the help-wanted sign than it did for the first person to come in to apply.

"Sapphire? Are you really looking for an assistant? I'd love to work here," a familiar, young woman said in a rush of excitement as she burst through the door.

"Hi, Desiree! I am looking for someone. Blade, this is Desiree. She's an art student who shadowed me for a week last semester."

"I'm glad to meet you, Desiree. I'll go check on the workmen and let you two talk." Blade nodded to the back door, and Sapphire understood the message. He was close.

"Come sit down, Desiree. Tell me about your availability." Sapphire invited her over, waving Desiree back to her workspace where she had two stools drawn up to the table.

"Taking the sign down already?" Blade asked later that morning when Sapphire untaped the announcement.

"She's perfect. Thank goodness, she'd come by to ask me a question about suppliers." Some of the stress heaped on her shoulders had disappeared after talking to the young woman. She continued, excited by the prospect of having help. "Desiree is going to start tomorrow. We're going to overlap shifts for a while, then I'll let her have some hours alone in the shop."

"I'm glad, Little girl. You've been doing a lot for a long time."

"I told her about that guy. I want her to be safe too," Sapphire said.

"I heard you. She didn't seem fazed by it."

"She'll be careful."

"And so will you. The door is fixed, and the cameras are functional. Are you ready to close the shop and get out of here early?" Blade asked, studying her face.

"I'm not going to let him win. Besides, he's out of the picture for a few days at least," Sapphire said and realized she meant it. She'd worked hard for this shop. Some guy wasn't going to make her run away from her dreams.

"Good girl."

She watched him go take a seat at the workbench and knew he'd stay with her for as long as she needed him. A warm feeling around her heart made her aware of how much she cared for him. Sapphire walked to his side and wrapped her arms around his waist.

"Have I told you how awesome you are, Daddy?"

"There's no limit on how many times you can tell me that, Blue Eyes." He rotated on the stool to lift her onto his lap. "I was scared today, Little girl."

"Petrified," she whispered.

"You did all the right things." He ticked her wise choices off on his fingers. "You called the cops. You phoned me. You stayed strong and didn't panic. I'm so proud of you."

"I walked right out into his hands," she said, shaking her head at her own stupidity. Blade hadn't said anything about that move.

"Did you check the cameras?"

"Yes."

"Was there anyone at the door?" Blade probed.

"No. I could see you all a distance away. I thought you were just looking at the aftereffects of that guy trying to break in."

"Now there's a wider lens camera back there. You can't anticipate everything that could happen, Little girl. You did all the correct things. He didn't. This is on him—not on you."

Staring at his face, Sapphire processed his words. He was right. She wasn't to blame.

"How did I get so lucky to find you?" she whispered.

"I don't know, Little girl, but I won't lose you now." Blade cupped the back of her head and pulled her close to kiss her gently.

Sapphire deepened the exchange. She'd seen her hero in action today, and he was so hot. Stroking his hard muscles, she reveled in his strength.

Blade broke off the kiss with a groan. "Little girl, I'd fuck you right here on your workbench, but I don't need spectators. Do you?" he asked as the bells on the door jingled.

She shook her head and peeked over her shoulder toward the open door behind her. Controlling the laughter that threatened to spill from her lips, Sapphire winked at him and called a hello to the customers. She didn't even care they'd caught her on his lap. Who wouldn't want to be that close to Blade?

Sliding off his thighs, she whispered, "Can I have a rain check for that?"

The heat in his eyes blazed hotter. She knew she was in for it when he got his hands on her in private. "You're playing with fire, Little girl."

"I can't wait. Go back to the shop, Blade. I'm fine here. I'll call if I need you."

"You sure, Blue Eyes?"

"Definitely. I'll send you text updates," she promised.

"Go help your customers. When I can stand without knocking things over, I'll take off."

"Without knocking things over?" she repeated and scanned

his body, trying to pinpoint what the problem was. Her gaze landed on his lap. "Oh!"

"Don't stare at it, minx. You're going to make it worse," he growled.

Giggling happily, she winked at him and headed over to take care of her customers. When she checked back a while later, the stool was empty. Sapphire missed him immediately.

Thankfully, the shop was busy. Time flew by. Sapphire had never been so grateful that Monday was one of her short days—and that was saying something.

She stood studying the exterior on the new camera for several minutes after she'd closed the shop. It was taking all her courage to walk outside. Finally, she wanted to get home so badly, Sapphire risked it. Opening the door into the artificially lit area, she stepped out.

Sapphire scanned the area and froze when she saw a man bracing his muscular butt on her car. "Couldn't you have stood in the light? That would have made it easier for me to come out of that back entrance."

Blade pushed away from the car and walked forward to hug her. "You'll find it less difficult tomorrow and less scary the time after that. Soon, you'll remember but not allow yourself to react. Eventually, you'll forget until you're on your way home...."

"Do you think that will happen?"

"Someday. There's no timeline. Trauma takes a while to fade."

"How did you get so smart?" Sapphire asked before pressing a kiss to his neck.

"I might have had a few negative encounters over the years. We should work on that idea of Ivy's to create something beautiful that has a hidden defense component," Blade suggested.

"I actually drew a few sketches today. I'd love to get your opinion of them—I don't think I've come up with a really good idea yet." Sapphire realized she'd forgotten where she was and how frightened she should be back here. "How do you make things so much better?"

"We're good together, Sapphire. I'll always be there for you," he promised, bringing tears to her eyes.

She swallowed hard before blurting, "I love you."

His lips widened in a breathtaking smile. "I love you too, Little girl." He pressed a soft kiss to her lips before deepening it.

Savoring his taste, Sapphire responded with all the emotions inside her. She wiggled closer, erasing the space between their bodies. His arm tightened around her waist, and one hand smoothed over her lower back to cup her bottom. Desire flared inside her. That hand lifted her to press her pelvis to his. Feeling the proof of his arousal, Sapphire wanted more.

She ripped her mouth away from his. "I need you, Blade."

"Let's go inside, Blue Eyes."

Their previous conversation zinged into her mind. He wouldn't. "The workbench?"

"I can't wait to see you stretched over it. Your sweet ass and pussy on display. Are you wet, Sapphire?"

"Drenched," she admitted, rubbing her mound against his thick erection.

"You have one job, Little girl. If our play scares you, tell me. Don't hesitate. Tell me. Promise."

"Yes," she said, understanding even as their passion exploded, he wanted to take care of her. "You have my word."

"Get the key," he demanded.

She loved his urgency. Digging in her pocket, she fumbled for her keys. Blade plucked them from her hand and quickly dealt with the lock. He swept her inside, secured the reinforced door behind them, and dropped the keys to the floor to free his hands.

He leaned over and scooped her up over his shoulder before she realized what he was up to.

"Blade!" she protested.

He answered with a sharp spank to her bottom without slowing. "Daddy."

Navigating through the darkness, he carried her through the crowded storage area at the rear of the store. His movements were sure and quick, as if he had the night vision of a predator. The shop area was lit with the last rays of sunshine filtering through the display window's security shutters.

Unable to resist the rounded butt in front of her eyes, Sapphire swatted it, only to shake her hand to deal with the resulting sting. "Damn that's hard."

"You, Little girl, are in big trouble," he growled, not faltering a step as he approached her design area.

The world spun around her as he set her back on her feet. She clutched his leather vest to stabilize herself. "Sorry?"

"No, you're not. But you will be," he said confidently as his hands ripped her T-shirt off and tossed it away.

She didn't look to see where it landed. Her gaze focused on his hungry expression. With a flick of his fingers, Blade unfastened her front-close bra. He didn't bother with removing that scrap of lace. He cupped her breasts and pushed them together, whisking his rough thumbs over her beaded nipples.

"Damn, you're pretty. A taste." He added to his compliment as if talking to himself.

Sapphire rose onto her tiptoes as he licked one nipple before sucking it into his mouth firmly. Her fingers tangled in his tousled hair, holding him to her. When he released the first with a pop, she moaned at the sensation. To her surprise, when he turned to the other side, Blade rolled that nipple between his teeth. The slight bite of pain sent a completely different zing of arousal through her. Sapphire tightened her grip on his hair, pulling him away.

"Good, hmm?" he hummed against her skin, allowing the vibration of his lips to brush the sensitive peak.

"I need you."

"Good. I'm going to bury myself so deep inside you that you'll remember me when I'm gone," he told her as he stood to unfasten her jeans.

His rough movements jostled her slightly, making her breasts rock. She loved that he rushed as if he craved making love to her. As soon as her fly parted, Blade thrust his hand down her opened jeans to cup her pussy. She knew he could feel how wet she was.

"So hot, Blue Eyes." His squeeze made her knees wobbly. She clung to his strength. Her desire built with every stroke of his fingers over her silky panties.

"Daddy," she whispered.

"I know. I can feel it too. We have a spanking to deal with first," he told her sternly as he put that hand to another purpose and yanked her jeans and the scrap of lace to her knees. "Daddies spank Little girls when they need an emotional outlet or a reminder to behave. I think you qualify for both."

"What? No!"

The room rotated as he spun her around to face the table. "You have ten seconds to shift anything you don't want under you."

Sapphire looked over her shoulder, trying to understand what he meant.

"Ten. Nine."

She whirled around to face the workbench, grabbing anything in front of her as his countdown continued. Pliers, wire, gems in storage boxes. Sapphire shifted them to the sides of the table to make room, not sure exactly what he would do. Paying attention to him seemed the prudent thing to do.

"Two." Blade picked up a pair of shears and relocated them to the side, helping her.

"One," he announced. "Time's up, Blue Eyes."

Gripping her waist, he lifted her to drape over the narrow table. Her feet dangled in the air as the wooden structure supported her torso. She didn't have a second to adjust when his first swat landed on her exposed bottom. Hampered by the jeans around her knees, Sapphire couldn't avoid the second stinging spank. She reached behind her, trying to shield her vulnerable buns, but Blade dealt with her hands easily. He captured her wrists and pinned them high behind her back.

"Uh, uh, Little girl. That's a no-no." His heavy hand continued to land. Each swat sounded in the quiet room and ricocheted through her mind.

Sapphire opened her mouth to yell at him and heard a feminine voice outside. "Crap. She is closed. I hoped I'd catch her before she left for the evening. We'll have to visit tomorrow. Sapphire has the most amazing—and original—jewelry."

"You have to stay quiet, Blue Eyes. Shhh!" he said, leaning over her body. For a split second, he allowed her to feel his weight pinning her down before he eased away. She loved the reminder of who dominated her.

She bit her lip, trying not to let any gasps or moans slip out. This was so naughty to play around in here. She'd never be able to look at the workbench without remembering this.

"Not a single word," he whispered.

"But...." She struggled to find something to finish that protest. Another stinging slap stole her breath and broke her control. An avalanche of emotions flooded from her. Tears coursed down her cheeks to land on the platform below her. A sob burst from her throat.

His hand smoothed over her hot skin. "Are you okay, Sapphire?"

"Hold me, Daddy," she pleaded.

In a flash, he'd rotated her to sit on the table in front of him. Her heated bottom pressed against the hard wood as Blade pulled her into his arms. A hiss escaped from her lips. He squeezed her tighter.

"Let it all out," he requested softly. "You've been too courageous today."

"I always have to be brave," she told him sadly.

"Do you feel that way with me, Blue Eyes?" he asked, and she could hear the sadness in his voice.

"No, I can relax and be myself when I'm with you. I'm glad."

She lifted her lips to ask for a kiss and enjoyed his masterful response. There was no doubt this man could kiss.

"Being with you makes my heart happy too, Little girl."

"Daddy? I need you to replace the bad memories in here with something I'll never forget." She rubbed her hands on his chest, aiming for a seductive look.

"Oh? That fits perfectly with my plans."

Squeezing her thighs together, she celebrated the heat rebuilding inside her. It felt amazing to feel good after the terror of the day. Sapphire wasn't ashamed of letting her emotions out. Blade understood. Maybe he'd deliberately pushed her a bit.

Holding her gaze, he yanked her jeans and panties completely off. Blade gripped her thighs and widened them. He stepped into the space he'd created and cupped the back of her head. Tugging slightly at her hair, Blade kissed her. The heated exchange made them both breathless. He lifted his lips from hers and scanned her body, allowing her to see his appreciation of her form.

"You are so beautiful, Little girl. I need a taste."

Blade trailed kisses down her sensitive neck to her collarbones. Sapphire loved the licks and nibbles that accompanied his explorations. She pushed back her shoulders to present her breasts to him.

"Look at these pretties. You're a temptation I can't resist." Blade growled and ran his hands up her ribs to lift each globe. He ran his tongue around her nipples before sucking on the taut buds as he caressed her soft skin.

Sapphire squirmed, loving every touch and wanting more. Needing to be in contact with him, she wiggled to the edge of the table to rub her pussy against his jeans. The combination of his touches and the rough fabric fueled her arousal.

"Daddy!" she whispered, not knowing what she needed but wanting it all.

"Shh! I've got you, Little girl." Blade lowered himself to his knees and pressed a kiss to her inner thigh.

She watched him turn to admire her spread open pussy. His eyes darkened, almost appearing black. His nose widened as he inhaled her scent. The animalistic act triggered her most basic reactions. Her juices gushed as she reached out to grip his shoulder. "Please."

"Not going anywhere."

His deep voice sent a shiver up her spine. She couldn't tear her gaze away as he leaned forward to press a kiss at the top of her cleft. Dipping his head slightly, he tasted her. His tongue ran through her wetness. Sapphire held her breath.

"Mmm," he hummed against her tender flesh, sending vibrations through her.

Sapphire felt like she was on a hair trigger. When he circled her clit with his tongue, she started to shake. She needed to come so badly. He wrapped his lips around that small bundle of nerves and sucked.

Sapphire slapped one hand over her mouth to muffle her sounds from the public she could hear moving around on the sidewalk, and her body exploded with pleasure. Blade continued his teasing touch, prolonging the sensations.

When she could think once more, Sapphire was covered with a fine sweat. She tightened her fingers on his shoulders. When he glanced up, she whispered, "Fuck me, please."

Blade pressed one last kiss to her mound before rising to his feet. The waistband of his jeans barely contained his cock. His arousal tented the heavy material. She reached forward automatically to help him. Their fingers fumbled together as he unfastened his jeans, allowing his erection to escape. She rubbed her fingers along the rigid shaft.

"You're going to be the end of me, Blue Eyes," he said as he grabbed a condom from his wallet.

Her gaze followed his movements as he lifted the small packet to his mouth. He bit down on one corner, to hold it. Blade brushed her hand away before easing the stretchy fabric of his athletic briefs off over the wide head pressing against it. He groaned when Sapphire licked her lips in appreciation.

Closing his eyes as if he struggled for control, Blade grabbed the waistbands and pushed his jeans and underwear to his knees. He retrieved the condom from his mouth and ripped it open. Immediately, he rolled it over his shaft.

Holding himself, he met her gaze. "Soon, I'm going to fill your mouth, but now I need to feel your pussy's heat."

Sapphire nodded and reached forward to tug him closer. "Now, Daddy."

He fit himself to her opening and flexed his hips, pushing slowly into her. She tried to hurry him up but couldn't speed up the process. She wrapped her legs around his waist and pulled him closer. His warning look made her heart flutter inside.

"Do I need to spank your bottom, Little girl?"

She shook her head instantly, even as her mind processed his words. Sapphire could only focus on the feel of his cock filling her as he continued to enter her. Slowly, her channel widened to allow him inside as he invaded. She guessed he was protecting her with the unrushed pace but didn't want to wait.

His thickness challenged her, but Blade finessed his way into her heat. Her reward? He brushed over so many sensitive spots inside her as he glided into her. Now the root of his cock pressed directly on her still-sensitive clit. He pulsed deeper in short thrusts, targeting that needy bud.

"Hold on, Sapphire," he commanded.

When her hands gripped his broad shoulders, he wrapped his arms around her in a tight embrace, pinning her to his hard body. Blade stood and turned around to reverse their positions. His cock pressed fully inside her as he sat down on her workbench. A strangled groan burst from her lips.

She clung to Blade. This was delicious to watch his cock slide in and out of her. Sapphire had never had such a bird's-eye view. Captivated by the erotic show, she lifted her knees onto the edge of the workbench. Sapphire bounced slightly and pressed her hand over Blade's mouth as he moaned loudly.

"Shh, Daddy!"

"Kiss me," he growled, pulling her close.

Eager to please him, Sapphire replaced her hand with her lips. Now to make him moan again. She concentrated on squeezing her intimate muscles, bringing an instant reaction from him. She absorbed his gasp and kissed him deeply. Her tongue tangled with his.

Their bodies moved together in almost harmony. Those awkward moments that always happened, making them both laugh and formed precious memories she'd never forget. *Remember that time you made love to me on my workbench and almost stapled your hand?* It was when that thought popped into her brain, Sapphire knew she wanted to keep Blade until they were old and gray.

"I like that idea that just went through your mind," he said, reading her expression.

She didn't answer him but lavished caresses on his hard body to show him how much she cared. As if he understood, he answered her loving touches with those of his own. *Damn. I love this man.*

The swirling sensations and emotions proved too much for Sapphire. Pleasure burst through her. Her deep contractions tempted Blade as well. Grabbing her hand, he placed it over his lips and shouted as he emptied himself into the condom inside her.

When he'd recovered, Blade swore, "I'm adding insulation to your walls, Little girl," and then returned the favor by covering her lips with his hand as she giggled with delight at his growly declaration.

Making love with Blade was indescribable. The perfect combination of skilled lover, tough biker, and loving Daddy Dom. She was never ever going to let him go. Blade seemed to fit into her life like a missing puzzle piece. He completed her in so many ways.

CHAPTER
TWELVE

"Blade, your girl just walked in," Ink alerted him.

Blade turned from answering Storm's question to spot her at the door of the clubhouse. Sapphire was worrying about something. The tightness around her mouth was a dead giveaway. Abandoning his beer, he stood up and walked to greet her.

"Hi, Blue Eyes. Did everything go okay this afternoon?"

"Hi...." She leaned in to whisper, "Daddy."

"Sweetheart, you don't have to talk quietly here," he reminded her.

"I know. I'm just getting used to calling you that around people," she confided in the same low tone.

"You take as much time as you need, Blue Eyes. What happened today?" he probed. They'd talked repeatedly throughout the course of the day. She hadn't allowed him to go to work with her again. He required her to call every two hours to check in with him—more often if she got scared. She'd followed his directions perfectly.

"Yes. I worked on one of the projects you brought me while Desiree was taking care of the customers. I love having her there. She's going to be a great help."

"Good. You needed an assistant."

"You won't believe this. My cousin, Amelia, came in to shop. She'd never visited before. She bought several pairs of earrings," Sapphire shared.

"And she was pleasant?" Blade asked.

"Yes. Unbelievably so. It was nice."

"Good for her. Maybe you can teach an old dog new tricks."

"Blade!" Sapphire slapped his thick bicep. He was always in her corner. She was going to remember that visual of her cousin as a snapping mongrel. That would make it easier to shake off any rude comments Amelia made. Fingers crossed Aaron would choose civility over rudeness as well.

"Back to our project. Are you going to share it with me?"

"It needs to be polished more, but you can see what it should look like," she said hesitantly.

"Show me, Little girl." He extended out his hand.

Slowly, she pulled her straps of her large purse off her shoulder. Easing it open, she searched inside. When Sapphire appeared to be struggling to balance her bag on one hand and scavenge inside with the other, Blade took the heavy tote from her and held it steady.

"Try finding it now, Blue Eyes. You don't need knives with this thing. One good blow and you'll knock someone out," he suggested.

"You!" she said with a laugh and searched again. "Here it is!"

After pulling out the protective package, she unwrapped it and handed over the metal item.

Blade stared at it, unable to believe his eyes. Finally, he put an arm around her shoulder and said, "Kitchen. I need light."

As they walked, she babbled, "I'm sorry. I tried to make it perfect. I think I can do better on the next idea if you're not happy with that one."

"I don't know what you're looking at, but this is more than I ever dreamed possible," Blade told her as he rotated it in the bright light of the kitchen. The detail work was amazing. It appeared solely decorative. Incorporated seamlessly into the design, the knives would create a visual that completely disguised their actual nature.

"Damn. I get the first order," Bear said, having caught a glimpse as he walked by. He stopped to examine it closer and then held out his hand.

"She's just slightly talented," Blade teased, as he handed over the implement for the biker to check out.

"Really? It's okay?" Sapphire asked, wringing her hands.

"I knew it would at a bare minimum be okay when I asked you to do this, Blue Eyes. This is more than I imagined. Hey! What's that?" Blade asked, pointing to a small embellishment at the corner of the design.

"I can take that off," she blurted. "It's our initials. BG for Blade Granby and SJ for Sapphire Jones. I thought because we worked on this together, we might want to add a credit for ourselves?"

"Hold this," Blade said to Steele as he walked by and slapped the unsharpened knife into the MC president's hand. He pulled Sapphire close and kissed her hard. Blade didn't know how she continued to amaze him, but she did. Every fucking time.

"Wow! This is amazing. Is this going in that fuel tank design? I need this," Steele said.

"That's what I said too," Bear added.

Blade waved them away behind Sapphire's back and concentrated on kissing her.

"Wait," Sapphire protested, wiggling back. "You guys like the design? It's not even polished yet."

"This is amazing, Sapphire. The customer is going to be so pleased. Blade's wait list is going to be two years long," Steele suggested.

"Let me see," Kade asked as he approached with his hand out. He looked up at Sapphire and said, "You do beautiful work."

"Thank you."

Kade locked gazes with Blade. "You're going to be swamped with orders, Blade. There's no way you can keep up with the demand there's going to be for these. I'd guess you have plans to make these embellishments on other spots on the bike?"

"Handlebars, frame… Yeah, I've got ideas," Blade admitted.

"What do you think about letting one of the apprentices start working with you?" Kade asked too easily. Blade guessed the shop manager had been planning to suggest this already.

As much as he hated giving up control of his specialty, Blade understood that, for the benefit of the MC, he needed to try expanding. "I get to choose." He felt Sapphire's startled response next to him. She knew how much he needed control.

"Of course. Got an idea now?"

"I do. But I think it's important to give anyone the chance to try out if they step up to the challenge. I bet I wasn't my teacher's first choice. It's only fair to pass along that opportunity," Blade told them.

"You want to announce it?" Kade asked.

"Nah. I'm busy here," Blade answered, looking at Sapphire, who stood in the crook of his arm.

"Gotcha. I'll return this when you're done celebrating," Kade told the two of them, wagging the decorated piece at them.

Kade glanced at Steele and Bear. "Come on. Let's see if we can get these guys to listen."

The trio took off toward the bar as Blade pulled Sapphire back against him. "You did so good, Little girl."

"Are you okay with having someone assisting you?" she asked, worried.

"Best thing I ever did was walk into your shop to see if we could collaborate. Working with one of the guys won't be as life-changing as finding my soulmate, but if I'm half as lucky, I'll end up with someone competent."

Sapphire bounced up on her toes to press her mouth to Blade's. After a soft kiss, she whispered against his lips, "Kiss me, Daddy."

He was more than willing to take over for her.

When they joined the gathering around the bar a few minutes later, Kade still stood on top of the wooden surface. Blade listened to the chatter as everyone discussed who would vie for the position. He had his eye on one guy.

Sapphire must have followed his line of sight. "Who's that?"

"Snake. He's new—came from an MC in Texas," Blade told her.

"He's who you want," she guessed.

"He is."

"Think he'll take a stab at it?" she asked.

The last word just popped from her mouth when the young biker shifted to look at Blade. Snake's eyes blazed with interest. He lifted his chin to acknowledge Blade's attention. Blade nodded once and turned back to Sapphire.

"He's in. Now, I'll see if he's as talented as I think. Steele's going to be pissed."

"Why?" Sapphire questioned.

"He's a welder."

"Isn't that what Steele does?"

"It is. But there's another new recruit who's got experience too. Steele can have him," Blade said.

"You really like the design?" she asked.

"I think I need a new tattoo."

"Really? Where are you going to put it?"

"Right over my heart, Blue Eyes."

"Can we go back to your room, and you can show me where?" Sapphire trailed a finger along his throat to the neckline of his T-shirt.

"I thought you'd never ask." Scooping her up into his arms, Blade strode down the hallway. He could answer questions and celebrate with the MC later.

Having his Little girl with him in the morning and the evening meant everything to Blade. Sapphire had been spending the night with him since the incident with that man. Peering over his cup of coffee at the woman sitting on the barstool in the MC's gathering room, Blade watched her face as he said, "I want you to move in here permanently with me."

"Give up my apartment?" she asked. "That's a big step."

"I want you in my arms every night. We could live at your place if you'd rather."

He watched her scan the large space. Several people were already up. Kade and Remi sat at a table, having breakfast together. He raised a biscuit to her lips, and she obediently took a bite. Her gaze focused on Gabriel moving around the kitchen to feed everyone. His Little, Eden, obviously had chosen to sleep in. A few single members sat in clumps around the room, drinking coffee and eating breakfast. The shop opened late on Sunday morning with a skeleton crew to take care of emergencies.

"I like it here. I have lots of new friends," she told him.

"So, we stay here. Want to keep your apartment for a while until you're sure you want to move in with me?" he asked.

"You sound so confident. You don't have any doubts, do you?" she asked. Her gaze assessed him carefully.

"I don't. I don't think you do either," he challenged.

She thought for a minute before confessing, "I don't. I love you and want to be with you."

"Then we live here together."

"It's that easy?" she asked.

"Yes. What do you want to do on your day off, Blue Eyes?"

"I'd like to do some designing with you. Then maybe we

could take a ride to get lunch? There's a seafood restaurant on Milligan's Lake I've wanted to go to," she suggested.

"I've heard of that place. Good plan, Little girl. Then a nap and playtime with your friends."

"I don't need to sleep during the day, Blade," she said, laughing.

"It's your day off. You need to rest. You're always so busy. I don't want you to run yourself down. You'll get sick."

"I'm never ill," she protested.

"I'm glad."

"You're still going to make me take a nap?" she asked in disbelief.

"With a red bottom or without. That's your choice."

She squirmed a bit in her chair. He could almost hear the gears in her brain churning away. "You have to lie down with me."

"Okay." Blade would stretch out with her in his arms. That certainly wouldn't be a hardship. He'd hold her any time he could.

The look on her face tempted him to laugh, but Blade controlled that impulse. He waited to see what she would say next.

"You were supposed to say no. Now I can't argue with you," she told him.

"Arguing with your Daddy is never a smart idea. Maybe you need to experience that naughty corner?" he suggested.

"I don't think I'd like that," she whispered.

"No, sweetheart. I don't think so either. So, some design work, a ride to lunch, a nap, and play with your friends?"

"Sounds like a great day," she said agreeably.

"Good girl. Now, let's finish breakfast and we can go brainstorm some new ideas."

That brought a genuine smile to her lips. As they talked about some concepts she already had, Blade knew she'd get used to him taking care of her. *One step at a time.*

CHAPTER
THIRTEEN

A raspy cough woke Blade. He glanced at the clock—three a.m. The hacking sound drew his attention back to the woman in his arms. Heat radiated from her. Concerned, Blade put a hand on her forehead. Sapphire was burning up.

A flurry of harsher coughs woke her. Blade drew her higher on the pillows. Sapphire pulled her teddy bear closer to her chest as she struggled to stop coughing.

"Let me get you something to drink," he told her gently before rolling away.

He was back at her side with cool water in her favorite pink sippy cup. "Here, Blue Eyes. Try this." Blade slid an arm under her shoulders to elevate her head.

She took several sips before sagging backward. "I don't feel well, Daddy."

"I'm sorry, sweetheart. You're burning up."

"I'm cold, Daddy. Can I have another blanket?" she said through chattering teeth.

"Of course, Little girl. Can you drink some more water?"

Sapphire shook her head and coughed again. "I'm sorry I woke you. Do you want me to go home?"

"You're home with me, Little girl. You're not going anywhere," he told her firmly.

"I don't want to make you sick," she whined.

That was just one more indication of how bad she felt. Sapphire never complained. She met everything directly.

"I'm not worried about me, Sapphire. I am concerned about you. Let's take your temperature."

"Okay," she said, opening her mouth before coughing.

"That's not going to work. Give me just a second. I'm going to grab a few supplies."

Blade pulled on a pair of jeans and headed to the door. The Shadowridge Guardians had created a closet near Doc's office that held all sorts of things for Littles. As he passed the medical room, Blade nodded. He might need to enlist the medic's help. Doc had treated a number of the Littles as well as the Guardians. Heavens knew the skilled man had stitched Blade up a few times. As he opened the closet, Doc came out of the treatment room.

"Is everyone okay?" Blade asked.

"Yes. I woke up and remembered I hadn't recharged a device. The last time I did that, I needed it urgently. Not wanting to tempt the fates, I came to plug it in. Is Sapphire okay?" Doc asked.

"I'm worried about her. She's got a terrible cough and is burning up but is shivering. I came out to get a thermometer."

"There's a nasty bug going around. Let me suggest a few things."

Doc opened the supply closet and handed Blade a large thermometer. "Littles should have their temperature taken in their bottoms. That's the most accurate way. Do you have lube?"

"Yes," Blade answered.

"Good. Use a lot. Here's a hot water bottle with a cute cover. Fill it with hot water and tuck it at her feet."

Doc rummaged around and found a box of liquid pain and fever reliever. "Give her the recommended amount of this every four hours as long as she has a fever. Measure by her weight. Grab the tissues with lotion. Those are good for delicate noses. I have some prescription-strength cough suppressant, but I'd need to examine her first. They're suppositories which are easier for a patient who's coughing."

Blade balanced all the items in his arms. "Thanks, Doc."

"You want to get as much liquid into her as possible. Take this." Doc grabbed a set of three colorful bottles. "Try different mixtures—juice, water, protein drinks. I'll suggest one more thing that helps Harper when her throat is sore."

Accepting the package of pacifiers equipped with a lozenge as the bulb to suck on, Blade nodded. "Good idea. That coughing has to make her throat hurt."

"If her temperature is over 102, get her in a cold shower. She won't like it, but keep her there until you can feel her skin cooling. Dry her and come get me."

"Got it. I owe you one," Blade said, so grateful that Doc had been there.

"Push my position up on your weaponry waiting list for some embellishments," Doc joked. "Really. Don't hesitate to knock on my door if you're concerned. I don't mind losing some sleep. The Littles are much more important than a few Zs." Doc patted him on the shoulder and returned to Harper.

Juggling all the booty he'd collected, Blade headed back to his Little girl. He could hear her coughing before he got the door open. Rushing inside, he found the bed empty. Blade dropped everything on the dresser and followed the concerning sound.

"Blue Eyes? Are you okay?" he said at the bathroom door.

"Daddy."

The weak response made him open the door and enter. Sapphire sat on the toilet with her head resting on her arms on the nearby vanity. He walked forward to brush her blue hair away from her flushed face.

"Let's get you back in bed."

She nodded slowly. "I ran out of energy."

"Daddy will help you." Blade quickly wiped her and flushed the toilet before scooping her up in his arms. Sapphire letting him care for her without protest was more proof that she felt awful.

Setting her on the mattress, Blade handed her Silver. "Daddy's going to check your temperature, Little girl. Let's roll you over on your side."

Blade shifted her position and pulled the covers over her shivering body. He quickly opened packages. Heading to the bathroom, he washed his hands and the thermometer before returning to her. She wouldn't like this. If he'd thought ahead, he would have introduced her to being cared for intimately.

Grabbing the lubricant from the nightstand, he coated his finger before turning back the covers over her cute bottom. He pressed her forward slightly and lifted her top buttock to expose her small entrance. Quickly, he applied the slippery mixture.

"Daddy. No. What are you doing?" she asked, coughs interspersed between.

"I'm checking to see if you have a fever," Blade told her as he pressed his finger inside the tight ring of muscles.

"No, Daddy. Stop!"

"Do you trust your Daddy, Little girl?" he asked, continuing to spread the lubricant inside.

There was a pause, and Sapphire nodded.

"Good girl." Blade withdrew his finger and inserted the thermometer deep into her bottom.

"Cold," she protested, trying to wiggle away.

"I know, sweetheart. It won't take too long."

She relaxed on the mattress as if struggling took more energy than she had. When ten minutes had passed, Blade removed the device and checked the temperature. 101. High but not at the panic state yet.

He wiped away the extra lubricant with a tissue and recovered her bottom. After cleaning his hands and the thermometer, he returned. Referring to the instructions on the liquid pain medicine, he measured out the correct amount for her weight. He'd carried her enough to have an educated guess.

Wrapping an arm around his Little girl, Blade helped Sapphire sit up. "I need you to take some medicine for me."

She sniffed the cup suspiciously. "That doesn't smell good, Daddy."

"Try holding your nose, Little girl. This will make you feel better," he promised.

To his delight, she followed his directions and pinched her nose closed. He placed the cup at her lips, and she drank all of it.

"Yuck, Daddy."

"Sorry, Blue Eyes."

"Tired, Daddy. Going back to sleep."

Blade kissed her temple. Quickly, he cleared the dresser. He washed the bottles and filled the hot-water bottle. Returning, he tucked that under the covers at her feet. Her sweet moan of enjoyment made him smile as he shucked off his jeans. Sliding in next to her, Blade wrapped himself around her, sharing his warmth.

"Daddy," she whispered and fell back asleep.

CHAPTER
FOURTEEN

Waking a few hours later, Sapphire heard Blade making coffee in the kitchen. Lured by the thought of a hot drink, she stirred in the bed. Her toes touched something soft and fuzzy. She immediately searched for Silver and found him napping on her pillow above her head.

She ran her toes over the object under the covers. What was that? Curious, she sat up and threw back the covers. Smiling at the cute owl that looked up at her, she pulled it toward her and heard it slosh. A water bottle. How fun!

"You must be feeling better," Blade observed from the doorway.

"Yes. I'll get up if you'll fix me some coffee."

"I'm going to check your temperature first. I think that medicine helped," he suggested.

A fit of coughing wracked her. Blade handed her cool water in a sippy cup when she stopped. "Try this."

The water soothed her throat. "Thanks. I guess I'm not totally recovered."

"Temperature. If it's high, you're staying in bed today," Blade decreed.

"Not possible. I have to open the shop," she said.

"Turn over."

When Blade picked up the thermometer case and lubricant, the memory of him caring for her last night rebounded into her brain. Sapphire squeezed her thighs together. That shouldn't turn her on. She'd never even considered anal play. It seemed so intimate. "You can take it in my mouth."

"You just drank cold water."

Crap. That would give a false report. She scrambled for another option. "You can use one of those forehead things."

"Little girls have their temperatures taken in their bottoms. Turn over."

From his expression, Sapphire knew arguing wouldn't help her. Slowly she rolled over onto her stomach. She pulled Silver close to hide her face.

"That's my good girl."

That phrase resonated inside her. She realized she wanted to please him. Sapphire also had to admit that submitting in this way aroused her. Not that she ever planned to admit that.

Blade pulled up the oversized T-shirt she wore to bed to expose her rounded buns. She shivered at the cold air wafting over her skin. Squeezing her eyes shut as he parted her buttocks, Sapphire tried not to react as he applied the slippery mixture to her tight opening.

This doesn't feel good!

Despite her attempt to keep him out, Blade slid a probing finger through that ring of muscle she clenched. Grabbing at anything to distract her from focusing on how much her body reacted to his touch, Sapphire recited multiplication tables in her head but totally screwed them up.

I should have listened closer in math.

"Daddy should pay more attention to your bottom. When you feel better, we'll start getting you ready to accept me here," Blade told her as he spread the mixture thoroughly.

"No, Daddy," she whined.

"Am I hurting you?" he asked.

She debated lying. Somehow, now didn't seem like a wise time. "No. I've just never...."

"Thank you for telling me, Sapphire. Daddy will take good care of your cute bottom."

Finally, he withdrew his finger and replaced it with the thick thermometer. It was cold inside her, making her shiver. The thought popped into her mind that she preferred his warm finger, and she moved her head, trying to shake it away.

"Shh, Little girl. Just a few more minutes," he promised, holding the instrument deep with a hand cupped over the end.

Finally, he removed it. She peeked to see him rotate the device. Blade shook his head.

"Still above normal. That medicine is keeping it down."

"So, I can go to work, right?"

"I'd rather you stay home, but if you think you're well enough to open the store...."

"I'm great," she rushed to tell him and coughed several times.

"You'll call me if you start feeling bad?"

"Yes!" she promised.

"And you'll drink lots of fluids and remember to take more of the fever medicine?"

"Definitely." She crossed her fingers under the covers.

"Desiree's there to help you today, right?"

"Yes. She's doing such a great job. She's there today and tomorrow," Sapphire shared.

"Let's get you dressed," Blade suggested.

"Thank you, Daddy," she said, sitting up and wrapping her arms around his neck. She had planned to head to The Blue Door whether he said yes or no, but it was easier if he cooperated with her.

Sapphire ate a few bites of yogurt for breakfast. It was cool on her throat and made Blade happy. He always insisted she had something before heading for work.

Everything seemed to sap her energy. By the time Blade

walked her out to the car, she felt awful. Stiffening her spine, Sapphire forced herself to look energetic like she was doing well.

"Are you sure you're okay, Blue Eyes? Tell me the truth," he asked as he helped her into her car.

"I'm good, Daddy. Don't fuss."

"Don't forget to dose yourself with more medicine at lunch," Blade reminded her. "Gabriel sent soup for you today."

"Thank him for me, please," she said before having a coughing attack. When she recovered, she smiled to reassure him through watery eyes.

"Call me if you need me."

She nodded and started the car. Sapphire concentrated hard as she navigated out of the parking lot and onto the road that ran along the front of the repair shop. Fits of coughing brought more tears to her eyes, and she even had to pull over once to find a tissue to wipe away the moisture clouding her vision.

Pulling herself together after parking in the rear lot, Sapphire scanned the area, making sure it was safe. Ever since that guy had caused such trouble, she'd been super vigilant. The walk to the back door seemed like a marathon. Sapphire locked it behind her and headed for her workbench.

Desiree's arrival a few minutes later required her to move to unlock the front door. Sapphire opened it and stepped away.

"I'd stay away from me if you can. I think I've caught something," Sapphire told her.

"You don't look good. Should you be here?" Desiree asked, before adding. "I should be okay with just about everything except handling the money. Why don't you set up the cash register and go home?"

"I don't want to dump my store on you, Desiree. That's not fair." Sapphire rushed to tell her.

"Fair, shmair. You won't feel better if you don't get some rest. Get the cash and we'll be ready to open. Then, let's call that hunk of yours and have him come pick you up," Desiree suggested.

"He'll be all growly and make me nap," Sapphire complained.

"I know. I'm so envious of you."

Sapphire stared at her for ten seconds before nodding. "I'm not going to make it."

"Do you want to phone him, or should I?" Desiree asked.

"I'll call. If you do it, an ambulance will be here to pick me up."

"Desiree, here's my phone number. Let me know if you have any problems. I'll be here before closing to take care of the register," Blade assured her at the back door. Sapphire leaned against him and didn't try to protest that Desiree could contact her. *Stick a fork in me—I'm done.*

"I'm definitely not poking you with utensils, Little girl," Blade informed her as he opened the passenger door to her car.

What? She'd said that out loud? How had she gotten over here? Weren't they talking to Desiree? Sapphire looked at the back of the building and found it abandoned. *I'm in awful shape.*

"You're right, Little girl. You are in awful shape. Doc's going to check on you when we get back to the clubhouse," Blade echoed her and Sapphire knew she'd spoken out loud again.

"I'll just go to sleep for a while. I'll be better when I wake up. I don't feel bad enough to see a doctor," she assured him. As if she'd jinxed herself, a horrible coughing fit descended on her. By the time she finished, she was crying.

"Blue Eyes. You're tearing my heart out. Let's get you home and on the road to recovery."

"Please," she whispered.

"There's water in this cup. Can you drink some?" he asked, holding out a blue sippy cup with a jeweled pattern.

If Sapphire had not been so miserable, she would have gushed over how cute it was. For now, she was more interested in the cold water inside. Taking a sip, she swallowed, letting the liquid soothe her throat. "Ah."

"I'm glad it tastes good. Can you hold it, or should I put it in the cupholder?"

Sapphire handed it to him. That was too much responsibility. She rested her head on the seat as he drove out of the parking lot.

"How are you going to get your bike home?" she asked.

"Kade drove me over. I'll ride my bike to your shop tonight to close up."

"What would I do without you?"

"I don't plan on you ever figuring that out, Little girl."

Time seemed to pass quickly because the next thing she focused on was the Shadowridge Guardians' complex. "Do you even know how to drive a car?" she asked.

Blade just laughed and squeezed her knee. She decided that must mean he did. Seconds later, Blade picked her up and carried her inside. "Aren't you supposed to be driving?"

"I'm all done, sweetheart. We're going to get you feeling better now," Blade assured her.

"That would be nice," she whispered, closing her eyes.

The clubhouse was fairly quiet as Blade walked through. A few people called out, asking if Sapphire was okay. Blade told them Doc was going to check on her. The positive support for that reassured Sapphire this was a smart idea. They all seemed to think a lot of Doc.

Blade carried her straight to the medical office. The door stood wide open. Blade entered and sat her on the exam table before positioning himself next to her.

Leaning against his hard chest, Sapphire glanced around the room. As sick as she was, Sapphire was amazed that it seemed like a doctor's office. "How often does someone get hurt?" she mumbled to Doc and his Little who appeared in the doorway.

"More frequently than you'd imagine," Doc told her before turning to Harper. "Go on, Little girl. I need to see how I can help Sapphire."

"Feel better, Sapphire," Harper told her cheerfully before lifting her lips for her Daddy's kiss. In a flash, she was gone, shutting the door behind her as she left.

"Sapphire, you look like you're suffering. What's going on?" Doc asked her.

A fit of coughing overtook her when she opened her mouth to answer. Doc immediately turned and got her a small paper cup of water.

"That's a terrible cough. Sip this slowly."

He held the cup as she drank, seemingly understanding that she had no energy. "Good girl. Does your throat hurt?"

Sapphire swallowed, testing it out and nodded. She didn't want to talk. That always made her start hacking.

"How are your ears?" Doc asked.

Sapphire shrugged. Everything hurt. She couldn't answer that question truthfully. Her assorted symptoms had coalesced into a horrid illness.

"How about if I just check you over? Okay?"

She nodded. That was much easier than having to think. Her brain was so fuzzy.

"Blade, let's get her undressed. From her shivers, she'll be better wrapped in a blanket as I examine her," Doc requested.

Before she had absorbed that statement, the two men removed her clothing. Doc took off her shoes and socks while Blade pulled her T-shirt over her head and unfastened her bra. Sapphire crossed her arms in front of her breasts to shield herself.

"No! What are you doing?"

Immediately, those words launched a coughing fit that zapped her last bit of energy. She drooped, propped up on Blade's chest. He rubbed her arm and back as he supported her.

"Blue Eyes, Doc has to examine you so he can help you feel

better. Do you get undressed when you go to the doctor's office?" Blade asked.

Shaking her head no, Sapphire tried to convince him.

"I don't believe that, Little girl. How long has it been since you were at the doctor's?" Blade asked.

It was hard to think, so she carefully held up five fingers, trying to keep herself covered.

"Five months?" Doc questioned.

She shook her head again.

"Five years?" Blade guessed.

Sapphire shrugged and nodded. It was probably over seven, but she wasn't going to tell them that.

"That means it was longer than that," Doc predicted. "You're due for a full physical when you're well, Sapphire. Let's check on that cough first. We need to get your clothes off so I can see if anything else is going on. You want to feel better, right?"

After hesitating for a second, Sapphire nodded. She felt lousy.

Immediately, the men finished the job. Blade laid her back on the exam table and turned her on her side before Doc draped the softest blanket ever over the top of her. Sapphire gathered a clump of the material in her hands and held it to her cold nose.

"Temperature first, Sapphire. Just stay still," Doc told her.

She knew what was coming. Doc pulled on gloves before applying cold lubricant to her bottom and spreading it around. Sapphire decided she much preferred feeling the warmth of her Daddy's touch instead. She shivered when he pressed the thermometer inside.

"I'm sorry, Sapphire. That's just too cold, isn't it?" Doc asked. His tone was sympathetic.

"He'd be a great Daddy," Sapphire told herself. Not as excellent as her own Daddy, of course, but she was happy for Harper.

When that ordeal was over, Blade lifted her into a seated position. Doc checked her nose, ears, and eyes before tugging her blanket away from her grip at her throat.

When she resisted, Blade leaned into whisper in her ear, "Be a good girl and let Doc examine you. If not, I will spank your bottom and then he will check everything needed."

Reluctantly, she let go of her death grip on the covers. He palpated her neck and looked at her throat. She could tell Doc was concerned by his expression when he listened to her lungs. That overrode her worry about him seeing her bare breasts as he pressed the stethoscope to different spots.

He pushed on her tummy and asked some questions about her stomach and periods. Sapphire was embarrassed and reassured at the same time. Doc was really good at what he did.

"If you'd waited another day to get medical treatment, you would have needed a trip to the hospital, Sapphire. You are very sick. At the brink of pneumonia. You are going to bed for at least forty-eight hours and not getting up for anything but to use the toilet. Can you do that for me, or should I have Blade take you to the emergency department?" Doc asked.

"But my store...." she croaked.

"I'll check with Desiree to see if she can pick up some additional hours. We can have some prospects with retail experience volunteer to staff it as well. Can you imagine how many women you'll have in the store if bikers are running it?" Blade asked.

She knew he was trying to distract her, but an image of muscular man candy stripped down to their leather vests and tight jeans burst into her head. There would be a stampede.

"Forty-eight hours. Okay?" Doc repeated.

Sapphire nodded. She felt so lousy.

Blade kissed her forehead. "Good girl. I'll make sure you get your reward when you're better."

"Blade, if Sapphire has trouble napping, try giving her a few orgasms. That usually works better than medication. We want her to sleep as much as possible. Let's move her back on her side," Doc suggested, helping to ease her back into position. "I'll gather some medicine for you. She needs a breathing treatment before she leaves."

Sapphire dozed as they talked. She woke up when Doc exposed her bottom once again, and she squirmed away. Blade immediately held her in position.

"Careful, Blue Eyes. You'll fall off the table," he warned.

"Your Daddy has some medicine for you, and I'm going to give you a shot. Which one do you want first?" Doc asked.

"Daddy," she croaked before coughing hoarsely.

When she'd settled back down, Blade spread her buttocks and pressed something cold into that tight ring of muscles usually hidden between them. "No, Daddy."

"This suppository is going into your bottom, Little girl. You're coughing too much to swallow a giant antibiotic," he said as he inserted the large medicinal dose deep into her bottom. "Relax for Daddy."

Sapphire forced herself to unclench her muscles and allow him to complete his task. To her horror, Blade confirmed with Doc, "Every two hours?"

"For the first forty-eight hours. Then, we'll see how she's doing," Doc stated. "Push liquids and give her light meals: soup, gelatin, ice cream. Anything that would soothe her throat."

"Just a little sting," Doc told her before lightly pinching her hip as he poked the needle into her bottom.

Tears popped into her eyes. She'd always hated shots. That one hadn't hurt too bad. "You're good at that," she croaked.

"I've had some practice." Doc patted Sapphire on the shoulder. "Feel better, Sapphire. I'll check on you."

"Thank you," she whispered.

Blade scooped her up in his arms, covered by the soft blanket. Doc opened the door and walked with them the short distance to Blade's room to help with that one as well. Sapphire saw Doc place a large bag of supplies on the kitchen counter as Blade carried her into the bedroom. Once settled in bed, Sapphire closed her eyes and tumbled into sleep.

CHAPTER
FIFTEEN

T wo days of recovery stretched to three. Sapphire felt better but knew she'd never make it through a long day at work. Talking still triggered her cough. Sighing deeply, she told Silver, "I want to get out of this bed. He can't keep me here, right?"

The gray bear looked back at her with a warning in his black eyes.

"I'm an adult, and I can get up whenever I decide." A wave of hacking resulted from her diatribe.

"Do I need to call Doc, Little girl?" Blade appeared in the doorway and crossed the room immediately to the bedside where he handed her water to drink.

Sapphire took a few sips before answering, "No. I'm okay. I need out of this bed. Maybe I could go hang out on the couch in the clubhouse."

"Not happening. Until your fever is gone, you stay here. Remember what Doc said—lots of naps. Sleep is almost as helpful as these," Blade told her, unscrewing the top of the suppository container he'd left right on the nightstand.

They were huge. How was that going into her bottom? Somehow, Blade always succeeded in administering her medicine.

"I don't want any," she said.

"I believe that. But you want to get better," he told her as he rolled her onto her side.

Extending her arms out, Sapphire tried to thwart his attempt.

"We've talked about this, Little girl. You will get your medicine until Doc gives the okay that you are recovered. Are you going to cooperate?" he asked.

"No." She shook her head and crossed her arms over her chest.

"Remember, you had a chance to make the right decision."

Blade pulled the covers away from her body and tossed them over the end of the bed. He plucked her off the mattress and sat down to drape her over his lap. Without saying anything, he spanked her. The first swat stung so bad.

"Ouch! Stop!" she demanded and coughed.

As soon as that spasm of hacking eased, he spanked her more. The next several swats came in a flurry. A heated sting echoed all over the tender skin of her bottom. Sapphire squeezed her thighs together, hoping he wouldn't see her reaction to the punishment. She felt drenched with arousal.

"Spread your legs, Little girl," Blade demanded.

When she slowly complied, he aimed his next whack directly on her pussy. That skyrocketed her desire. He repeated that move a second time, drawing a deep moan from her lips. The next spank landed on her buttocks again with a wet sound.

There's no way he missed that.

When her bottom was on fire, she abandoned struggling. "I'll behave," she whispered. That punishing hand switched to smoothing over her stinging skin.

"Thank you, Little girl. Now, let's see if Daddy can help you fall asleep."

Blade lifted her off his knees and tenderly returned Sapphire to her nest of pillows. He grabbed one of the soothing pacifiers and placed the lozenge into her mouth. She sucked on it furiously as he opened a drawer in the nightstand and removed a long wand vibrator. She hadn't seen that before.

"Doc says orgasms make a Little girl relax and go to sleep. Maybe we should see if Doc knows what he's talking about."

Sapphire shook her head, torn between embarrassment and arousal. He was going to make her come? And just watch her?

Blade pushed a button on the base of the device, and it hummed. He adjusted it to a less urgent pace and ran it over his muscular forearm. "There we go. That's a good relaxing level. What do you think, Sapphire?"

He took her hand gently and opened it so her palm rested on his. It was warm. From spanking her? She shivered at that thought. Sapphire watched him bring the vibrator close. He touched the tip to her palm first to judge her reaction. She looked up at him and discovered he watched her carefully.

"Is that good?" he asked.

Sapphire couldn't lie. It was as if that humming vibrated all the way through her. She shifted restlessly on the mattress. He moved the wand, running the tip from her index finger up her arm and across her collarbones. Sapphire arched her back to offer her breasts for his attention. Blade indulged her and traced the wand over her oversized T-shirt. He circled her breast, avoiding the nipple as he ran consecutively wider circles.

Clenching the covers tightly in her hands, Sapphire cried out, "No" when the vibrator lifted from her skin and shifted to torture the other side. Her muscles were so tense as she waited to see where he would tantalize next. She inhaled sharply as he drew it down her torso and over her stomach.

"Raise your knees, Blue Eyes, and place your feet together," Blade ordered as he dipped the vibrator under the hem of her T-shirt and scrunched it up as he traced a path on her thigh. "Good girl. Now drop your knees to the bed."

Cool air whisked over her most intimate area as she moved into the position he wanted. It made her aware of how exposed she was to his view and yet still so covered. Only her pussy was on display.

He rubbed the vibrator on the mound between her thighs. Already so turned on, she held her breath, in anticipation of what he would do. When he trailed the tip down her inner thigh and held it a fraction of an inch from her, she could feel the vibration of the air between the vibrator and her pussy.

"Please," she begged.

He paused, as if thinking. Sapphire realized she held her breath. She inhaled and froze as he slid the end of the vibrator through her wetness. Blade drew a line around her entrance and over her clit as she struggled to hold still.

"You are being so good. Let's try this to see if you like it." Slowly, he pressed the wand into her.

The vibrations launched sensations throughout her pelvis. She needed just a bit more. Bucking her hips up toward him, Sapphire tried to adjust the device to have it touch where she needed it to.

Blade slid it from her. She looked up at him in shock. He wasn't going to leave her here, on the brink of an orgasm, was he?

He lifted the vibrator to his lips and licked her juices from the tip. "Mmm. Little girl, you taste so sweet. I wonder if you'll taste the same or better after three orgasms?"

Her eyes widened as her brain seized on one part of that statement. "Three?"

His slow smile did things to her inside. She watched his face as he once again slid the device to her pussy. Hunger carved itself into his features as he sought to give her pleasure. The growing tension inside her drew her attention away from his handsomeness.

Sapphire's eyelids drifted to half-mast as he circled her clit. As if knowing direct pressure would be painful, Blade teased her with close brushes to the small bud. Suddenly, it became too much, and the sensations burst inside her body. Her hips rose to meet the vibrator and then crashed to the mattress.

Peering through mostly hooded eyes, Sapphire watched Blade lick the plastic. A second passed as he appeared to compare flavors. It was so hedonistic. She loved how sensual Blade was. Nothing would be off-limits with him.

"Hmm. I need more data," he told her and inserted the vibrator deep into her pussy.

The sudden burst of vibrations as her first orgasm weakened made Sapphire cry out as the sensations spread to her core. Blade held it deep inside, rotating the base to graze that sensitive bud he'd already teased. An orgasm hovered just out of her reach. A needy sound escaped from her lips.

"I'll make it better, Blue Eyes," he assured her. "Put your hands on the pillow behind you." With his free hand, Blade helped her stretch her arms over her head and rest them on her pillow. He pressed them into the soft padding, he instructed, "Keep them there."

When she nodded, he released his hold before leaning over her form to draw one of her taut nipples that pressed against her T-shirt into his mouth. The material became damp quickly as he sucked on that small peak. He lifted his head to blow a warm stream of air over that impudent nipple, making it contract even harder. Blade covered her breast with his palm to warm it while he repeated the process on the other side. The feel of his warm skin, mouth, and breath caressing her combined with the humming action at her core to spark a stunning orgasm that shook her.

Blade extended her pleasure once again before sliding the vibrator from her tight passage. It emerged with what seemed like a sea of her juices. She watched to see if he would repeat his actions. He did.

Pulling the gadget away from his tongue, Blade smiled. "Two is even better. Mmm! I can't wait to sample the third."

She didn't know what to say, so Sapphire stayed quiet, eager to see what he would do next to her.

"I'll need your help, Little girl. Give me your right hand," he requested holding his out.

Slowly, she lifted her arm from the pillow, not understanding what he wanted her to do. She placed her hand on his extended palm. He gently guided her fingers to her mound. Sapphire looked at him in shock. What was he asking her to do? "Daddy?"

"Help your Daddy, Blue Eyes. Stroke yourself the way you enjoy private time."

With her gaze locked on his deep brown eyes, Sapphire's face heated and she knew she was blushing furiously. "Touch myself?"

"Yes, Little girl. Show me what you like." His voice was low and growly with arousal but still held steel determination. He wasn't teasing. He was ordering.

Slowly, she moved. Stroking her fingers along her lower lips, she watched his eyes shift from her face down her body to the movement between her legs. The eroticism of doing this while he observed was tantalizing. Only with him did she have the courage to please herself in front of a lover.

Blade pressed the vibrator to the back of her hand. The device's tremors flowed through her fingers onto her skin, making her eyes roll up in her head. Every whispering brush of her fingertips sent shock waves through her. She'd played with vibrators before, but the combination of him as a spectator and the device made everything more potent, more exciting.

Tingles heralding her orgasm gathered. She bit her lip, trying to delay them. She didn't want this to end.

"Come, Blue Eyes. Let Daddy see your pleasure."

Blade traced his fingers down one leg from her knee to her core, dipping two shallowly into her. When she gasped, he pressed them deep inside her. He rubbed a magic spot on the wall of her tight passage, and those tingling sensations intensified. Sapphire brushed over her clit and tapped once. She shook with the force of her climax.

The vibrator's hum cut off. Her eyes flew back to Blade's handsome face. Those tantalizing fingers slid from her. Her juices shimmered on his skin. Blade lifted those wet digits to his lips in an erotic move that was so hot, she knew she'd never forget this moment. With a hum of enjoyment, Blade tasted her essence.

He seemed to consider his decision for a few seconds as he devoured the wetness coating his digits. She couldn't believe how intimate it felt as their gazes met.

"Three. I'll choose this as my favorite." Blade readjusted himself in his jeans, drawing her attention to the huge bulge there.

"I could help," she offered.

"Next time," he promised and drew the covers over her, tucking the edges under her chin. Blade leaned over and kissed her forehead. "Nap, Little girl."

Closing her eyes obediently, Sapphire knew she'd never get to sleep after all that. She heard him moving quietly around the room. Her body relaxed completely in her warm pile of blankets. Everything faded away as she fell asleep.

CHAPTER
SIXTEEN

Two weeks later, Sapphire had recovered fully. Blade had allowed her to go back to her shop after a couple of days. She'd reported that The Blue Door's babysitters had done an amazing job at selling her stock. She still had women coming in looking for some of the bikers who'd helped out.

Unfortunately, they'd gotten word while she was ill that the police had freed the man who'd attacked Sapphire because of a technicality. With her now back at work, Blade made frequent trips to the shop to make sure his Little girl was safe and happy. He knew she was jumpy and waiting for her attacker to return. He hated for her to feel this way.

With her at the clubhouse, Blade could relax. Sapphire would be safe here. He watched her hanging out with the other women a short distance away. She seemed to have fun with her companions.

Blade spent time with his Shadowridge Guardian brothers at the bar. The MC had welcomed Sapphire, and Blade knew they would do anything to protect her—as he would act to ensure the other Littles were safe. When Kade nodded, signaling him to step to the side, Blade followed him to a more private spot.

"I found your guy," Kade said under his breath as he handed Blade a note with an address. "He lurks here."

Blade glanced at it and nodded. "Thanks. I owe you one."

"I'll collect later. You protect your Little girl."

Blade stuffed the note in his pocket and turned to look at the library room entrance. Several Littles had disappeared inside for what they called official business. When Sapphire had hesitated to join the group, Ivy had linked her arm with Sapphire's and guided her into the gathering. Sapphire had peeked over her shoulder to meet Blade's gaze. Her huge grin celebrated her inclusion.

He would pay the man a visit soon.

"Blade! He's back. I can see him outside the rear door. I've called the cops."

"I'm on my way," Blade said, dropping his wrench with a ringing bang as he ran for his bike. He didn't have to say a word. Ink and Snake followed him.

When they arrived at the rear of the jewelry store, Blade scanned the area. The man wasn't there. He knew that Sapphire hadn't imagined it. The guy must have fled when the sound of the motorcycle engines revving reached him.

The back door burst open, and Sapphire ran outside. "He was here. He left just as I heard you coming."

"It's okay, sweetheart. Look. Here's the police," Blade pointed to the squad car that appeared in the parking lot.

In a few minutes, the squad car left the parking lot. They'd taken a copy of the security cam footage and would add this to the case against the would-be intruder.

"Nothing can stop him. I'm just a sitting duck here. What can I do?" Sapphire asked, distraught.

"You're going to be vigilant and stay safe. He'll mess up long before he hurts you, and no technicality will save him that time," Blade promised, wishing he could make that the truth.

He spent the rest of the afternoon at The Blue Door with Sapphire. Blade distracted her with the design to address Ivy's wish for a protective piece of jewelry that would be beautiful as well. In a flurry of sketches and adaptations, the artist and the weaponry expert both contributed their talents to create something a woman would love to wear with a secondary use of keeping her safe.

As they left at closing time, Blade was glad to find Sapphire was excited to focus on the new idea. She had already decided to make them for all her friends, so they'd be safe as well, but Ivy would receive the first one. Sapphire had already started to build the mold to create the components. Then they'd only need a chain, and Sapphire had plenty of those in stock.

Her enthusiasm had continued through bedtime. He'd tucked her in and then stretched out next to Sapphire to help her fall asleep. As soon as he could tell from her breathing that she slept soundly, Blade crept away from the bed and out of the room.

Kade approached as Blade walked through the clubhouse to get to his bike. "Need backup?"

"I'll do better alone so I don't alert him. Can I count on you to keep an eye on Sapphire?" Blade asked.

"Definitely," the large man assured him.

"Thanks."

Blade turned and stalked from the room. Already focused on what he would need to do, he jumped on his bike and guided his motorcycle out of the parking lot. A lot of people still traveled on the roads, but as he neared the location Kade had reported the scumbag slunk to at night, the streets emptied. No one wanted to hang around this area—especially in the dark. No one, of course, but someone on a hunting expedition.

Blade parked his bike several blocks away and left his cut on his seat as a warning to anyone who might consider stealing his ride. He moved silently through the streets. Following Kade's directions, he located the abandoned building where one Albert Jacobs spent his nights. He moved quietly through the rooms, checking on several people sleeping to locate his target.

In a back room, he found him. Blade pulled a knife from his jeans and crept close. It took all his self-control not to end the scumbag who had threatened Sapphire. With the sharp edge held to Albert's throat, he nudged him awake. "Make a noise and I won't give you a chance," Blade promised.

"You're that guy with the earring lady," the man said hoarsely.

"That's right. You're going to forget she exists and take a bus out of town. I'll give you three days to make the wise decision to move elsewhere. And, of course, you'll never come back."

"I'm not leaving. I know people here," Albert answered.

"You're a pleasant fellow. You'll charm new friends," Blade said sarcastically.

"I have rights. You can't force me get out of town."

"You're not too smart, are you?" Blade asked, pressing his knife tighter to Albert's neck. "How's the wrist?" he asked, nodding at the filthy bandage that clung to the man's skin. "I could have killed you with that throw. You cause her even a second of distress and I'll aim much differently."

"I'm not afraid of you."

"Or I might just decide that she would sleep better at night after your friends find your body in an alley somewhere. That's always a risk."

"You're just trying to scare me," Albert said with bravado that didn't quite erase the fear in his eyes.

"No. If frightening you was my goal, I'd draw your attention to the other knife I'm holding next to your dick." Blade flexed his fingers slightly, allowing the other man to feel the sharp tip.

Blade didn't think it was possible for more of the whites of the man's eyes to show. He was wrong. "You've got three days.

I've even made your life easier by buying you a nonrefundable ticket to the location of your choice, at least two hundred miles away."

The man looked at him with way too much defiance. Blade knew he'd need convincing. "Oh, I should warn you to keep your guard up against any possible threat. I'll be sure to remind you of our chat tonight from time to time."

Flexing his hand by the man's crotch, Blade sliced through the filthy jeans and opened a shallow cut. His sharp blade accomplished that so easily that his target didn't feel anything. He'd notice tomorrow when he woke up to find his pant leg was blood soaked. The ticket was inside the man's coat. That would make Albert wonder how Blade had accomplished that without waking him.

He walked to the door, hearing Albert scrambling behind him. Blade kept to the shadows and climbed to an elevated position. Just as he'd expected, Albert followed him. Blade tossed a sharp knife toward his target, causing Albert to jerk back as the edge grazed his nose on its path before thudding into the wooden fence beside him.

With a string of expletives, Blade's target turned and ran, retracing the route he'd come from.

Thud.

Albert stopped in his tracks as a knife landed between his feet in the alleyway. He looked up and shook his fist. "You can't scare me. I'm not going anywhere."

Blade disappeared as he laughed soundlessly. He'd had no idea this would be so fun.

Later that day, he stopped Albert in his tracks when the violent man passed the small bakery three doors down from The

Blue Door. The beleaguered man discovered a knife pinned his unworn hood on his sweatshirt to the wooden siding. Blade enjoyed the man's panicked thrashing when the garment choked him as it pulled against his neck.

The voice of Albert's companion drifted to Blade as the younger man ran. "They told me someone's after you. Keep away from me."

It seemed the word was out. No one wanted to be around Albert. They all thought Blade would have to miss and hit someone soon. They didn't realize he never missed.

"Fuck!" Albert screamed a couple hours later when the sandwich he lifted to his mouth exploded. He turned to find a single slice of salami tidily tacked to the wall with an ice pick.

By that evening, Albert was on a one-way bus headed to Toledo. Albert never saw the employee in the ticket booth send a notifying text, revealing his destination. The Shadowridge Guardians MC had a lot of friends in town. Blade would alert a motorcycle club in that city to be aware of him when he returned to the clubhouse. After hiking back to his bike, Blade swung his leg over the seat. He'd have some explaining to do to his Little girl.

The MC wouldn't ask questions. He figured Kade had a good idea of what he was doing. Blade had already arranged for Snake to take over for him in making some of the components for the latest build. His prospect needed time to work independently.

Sapphire would have a lot to say.

"What do you mean you watched my attacker get on a bus to Toledo?"

"That's the good news, Little girl. He's gone and should be

out of our lives," Blade assured her. He carefully controlled his expression to squelch the smile that would reveal his amusement.

"You left me in the middle of the night and didn't answer any of my calls. I thought something had happened to you. The guys in the MC seemed to know more than I did, but they wouldn't tell me anything," she ranted.

"I'm sorry, Blue Eyes. I wasn't in a place where I could pull out my phone. You wanted me to be safe, right?"

"That means you were in danger. That isn't acceptable. Especially because I guessed you were dealing with that menace to society," Sapphire accused him. Each word that emerged from her mouth was louder than the previous one. She was totally out of control.

"Don't yell at me, Sapphire. You can be upset with me without shouting. It's important for you to remember that I can take care of myself. I was not in danger, and I wouldn't put myself in peril. I have way too much to live for, Little girl."

"I can yell if I want," she answered at the top of her voice.

"You can. Your throat may not be too happy with you in a few minutes. I know your ass won't be," Blade told her calmly as he walked into the bedroom.

The other room was quiet as he pulled out the toy drawer. Sapphire was listening. Purposefully, he rattled several things inside as he gathered a plug and the lubricant. Returning, Blade watched her gaze settle on the items he held.

"I don't have to wear that," she said quickly.

"I thought I'd get it ready if you wanted to continue ranting."

"I have the right to be angry," Sapphire told him, her focus narrowing in on his face.

"Why exactly are you upset—because I put myself at risk?" Blade asked, tapping the base of the plug on the counter.

"Yes! You should have left everything to the police. They get paid to handle bad guys."

"They have to work within parameters. I don't have any

barriers," Blade explained. "I'm not always a good guy, Blue Eyes. Sometimes the situation demands a much different approach than the law would allow."

"Like this one? What did you do?"

"Not much. I harassed him a bit. He made the decision to leave."

"A bit," she repeated sarcastically. "What did you do? Carve him into small pieces?"

"Not quite."

"That doesn't reassure me." She propped her hands on her hips and stared at him.

She was so cute Blade struggled not to smile. Enough of Albert Jacobs. "He left town on a bus of his own free will. He's gone. Do you want to keep rehashing this or shall we stop thinking about that asshole?"

Sapphire's jaw dropped as she digested his suggestion. Finally, her shoulders sagged back into a more relaxed position and the anger dissipated from her face as she realized it was over. "I don't have to keep looking over my shoulder?"

"It's always smart to be aware of people around you."

"Everybody else likes me," she whispered.

"Of course they do. You're a sweetheart, Blue Eyes."

"I don't like that you put yourself in danger."

"I can't change who I am, Sapphire. No one messes with my Little girl." He walked forward and hugged her close. Blade felt her muscles relax as she leaned into him. "I love you, Blue Eyes."

"I love you, too, Daddy. I promise. No more time wasted on Albert Jacobs."

"That's my good girl. What did you do today at work?" he asked, changing the subject.

"I made a prototype for a necklace weapon," she shared. "A new idea popped into my mind."

"Can I see it?"

Sapphire stepped away to rummage in her large purse and pulled out a plastic pouch. Opening it carefully, she extracted her creation. When Blade held out his hand, she placed it gently on his palm.

Blade lifted it. The piece was delightful. "Everyone is going to want this. You've captured such a great expression on his face."

"I thought I could make them in different colors. Ivy's bear is Lucky. He's golden brown. I got this as close to that color as I could from my memory. I might have to tweak it a bit."

"I bet it's perfect. Does pressing the nose work?" he asked. The mechanics of creating a push button release for the blade had been tricky.

"Try it," Sapphire challenged him.

One firm touch to the enamel bear's nose and the ears separated from the top of the head. As he pulled that section free, a long blade appeared, forming a T shape from the bear-ear handle. Blade wrapped his fingers around the teddy bear's ears with the blade extending freely.

Lifting it, the simple design felt good in his hands and would be very effective for both slashing and stabbing. "This is unbelievably cute and lethal. No one would expect that this would be a self-defense gadget. Shall we show Ivy? See what she thinks?"

"Yes. Let's go."

"Not before this plug is in place," Blade reminded her, tapping the plug on the countertop again.

"I can't wear that out there," Sapphire refused with a shake of her head.

"You can and will. This will remind you who's in charge."

"But...." His Little girl swallowed hard before continuing, "I don't want to."

"I know."

"You could just give me a pass this time. Forget that I yelled," she suggested.

He shook his head. "That won't help you make better decisions in the future."

"And that will?" she asked, waving a hand toward the plug.

"Yes."

Her gaze focused on the metal object in his hand. Blade watched her expressions and tracked the thoughts he could read floating over her face. Defiance. Reflection on her actions. Acknowledgement of his dominance. Resignation mixed with titillation. If he had to make a bet, Blade would put all his money that she was already wet with desire.

When her eyes lifted to meet his, he knew she was ready. "Come here, Blue Eyes. Let's put your plug in and we can go hear everyone's squeals of excitement."

When she approached, he dealt with her jeans and panties before turning her around to lean over the counter. His palm smoothed over the rounded curves of her bottom. "Such a pretty Little girl," he whispered to her and watched her relax on the hard surface.

Blade lubricated her bottom well and slid the plug into place. As she wiggled in position, he pressed a hand to her lower spine. "Stay here. Daddy will help you get dressed in just a minute."

"Yes, Daddy," she answered, completely in Littlespace mode. "Can we put a bow on Ivy's necklace?"

"Of course. I think there is a fun gift bag and bows in the supply closet. Should we check there on our way?"

"That would be so fun. She'd like that," Sapphire assured him.

"Stand up, Blue Eyes, and we'll go see."

"Ooo!" Sapphire looked at him in shock as she rose and moved around.

"An excellent reminder, isn't it?"

"Daddy!"

"We'll go slowly."

Blade hid his amusement as she walked in tiny baby steps to the door and across the hallway to the supply closet where the MC kept their special supplies. Sapphire immediately pointed to a new hair bow sitting on the shelf that was labeled with her name. "Look, Daddy."

"I think that's for you. It's the same color as your eyes." Blade clipped back a section of her hair with the new decoration and declared it perfect. "Should we go see who we should thank for that?"

"Yes, but Ivy's present first." Sapphire wouldn't allow herself to be distracted from her mission.

Blade appreciated whoever had thought of adding cute gift bags. Sapphire chose one with green butterflies on it and carefully tucked the necklace in its plastic pouch inside. She held on to both his hand and the handle as they strolled slowly down the hallway. He had a feeling a distraction would help keep her mind from focusing on the plug in her bottom. Only time would tell.

When they reached the group of eight Littles sitting at one of the tables playing spoons, all the women jumped up to hug Sapphire.

Remi asked, "What's that for? A present from your Daddy?"

"It's for Ivy. My Daddy and I designed it for her," Sapphire said nervously as she held it out to Ivy. "I hope you like it."

"You didn't have to get me something," Ivy said as she reached for the bag. "What is it? Oh, look, everyone. It's a teddy bear. It's just like the bear on the Shadowridge Guardians' cuts."

"Let me show you what it does," Sapphire offered. "You press the bear's nose, and this slides away. Then you hold that piece like this. Be careful. It's sharp."

"You remembered and made me something to wear that could protect me. What do I do with it if someone attacks me?" Ivy squealed, looking at Blade. Her voice attracted the attention of the other MC members, who crowded around.

Blade suspected his smile was as big as his Little girl's. Ivy's reaction and excitement was contagious. Sapphire had put so much into this design. He was proud of her.

"It works to stab or slash. Now, if you feel scared, pull this and have it ready. You can use your hand to cover what you're doing. You're just fumbling with your necklace," Blade told her.

"If you don't need it, you can put it back. If you do, you're ready. Don't be hesitant. Strike out with determination. Be a warrior."

Ivy nodded. A slow smile spread over her lips. "It's the same color as Lucky." She carefully put the ears back into place before holding it out to Sapphire. "Will you put it on me?"

"Sure. Turn around." Sapphire fastened the chain. "There you go."

Ivy whirled around to hug her tight. "Thank you so much!"

Blade watched Sapphire's eyes widen as the appreciative Little jostled Sapphire's body. That plug was making itself known.

She gathered herself quickly to answer, "I'm glad you like it. I thought I would offer to create more necklaces. That is, if you would each like one? I can make them without the detachable weapon if you're more comfortable that way."

"I'm going to recommend that every Little should have a device to defend themselves. I'd like to see this original design for everyone, but their Daddies may have other ideas," Steele suggested.

The MC members nodded their agreement—even those without Littles.

"You never know where you'll be when something crappy happens. I'd like one with the self-protection feature," Molly stated. "Could it also have a pin to secure it?"

"Of course. I can add that," Sapphire assured the group. "That's a great idea. Then you can put it wherever it's best for you. Even inside a pocket."

Blade watched the women gather close together as they discussed all the possibilities. Their chatter focused on different colors to match their stuffies. He hated that this was necessary but loved how Sapphire had combined something dear to them with a secondary use.

"You could make a million dollars on those," Ink pointed out.

"It's worth a million to keep our Littles safe," Blade assured him. "I wonder who's next to find their Littles?"

"Maybe King? He's seemed distracted lately. He's definitely been spending his time somewhere else," Steele observed. "We'll find out soon enough. Are you still planning to empty Sapphire's apartment tomorrow?"

"Yes. She's ready to stay permanently," Blade told him.

"Perfect. You got lucky, Blade," Kade said.

"That's definitely true. I'm not letting her go. She's one of us," Blade told the men.

They turned to look at the gathered Littles all animatedly talking. No drama. No competition. The Littles' relationships with each other were strong. These were their confidants and greatest supporters. Knowing his Little would have these incredible women in her corner reassured Blade. She was safe here.

As he watched, the Littles checked in frequently toward their men. Blade sensed their relationships with their Daddies were forged with heat and genuine love. Seeing the Littles with their Daddies over the last months had proved beyond a doubt that their feelings were deep. He'd never known how much he could care about someone until Sapphire had appeared in his life.

He glanced at the men gathered in the clubhouse and suddenly felt very lucky. Not many people found a group that accepted them as they were—without reservations. His brothers in the Shadowridge Guardians meant more to him than his blood relatives.

"Daddy! You're so serious. Is everything okay?" Sapphire asked, wrapping her beautifully tattooed arms around his neck.

Blade wrapped his arms around her, pulling his Little close. Her gasp made him smile. She was definitely sensitive to that plug. "Everything is better than okay. The guys are going to help get you moved tomorrow. Do you still want to bring your furniture here to fill an empty room? At some point, a guest or one of the new members will move in there."

"I'd love it if a Guardian could use a bed or a battered couch. My stuff isn't very good," she said and bit her lip.

"No worries, Blue Eyes. Your things will help someone settle in here. A bit worn is fine. If it was too fancy, the bikers would be afraid to sit on it."

That mental image brought a giggle to her lips—and another quick inhale.

"I think your reminder has done its job. Let's go back to our apartment and I'll show you how much I love you, Little girl."

"I'd like that, Daddy."

CHAPTER
SEVENTEEN

Sapphire scanned her empty apartment. It was a visual reminder of how much her world had changed since Blade walked into her jewelry store. A crew of the MC members had shown up in trucks and on bikes. That had garnered a lot of attention from her neighbors.

A laugh bubbled out of her throat. She imagined what she would have thought if she'd not known all the bikers. They looked rough and dangerous. They were. But they were also the best guys to have in your corner. Not many people in the world would put their lives on the line for someone else.

"Everything good, Little girl?" Blade asked.

"Yes, Daddy. I'm the best I've ever been. I can't believe they cleared out my apartment in a couple of hours."

"The guys have headed back to the clubhouse. Is there anything else you need to do here?"

"No. I'm just thinking about how different life is now," Sapphire confessed.

"Different good or different bad?"

"Definitely good," she said, smiling at him. Sapphire loved that he always checked to make sure she was happy.

"I'm glad, Blue Eyes. I feel the same way. Let's get Silver and head home," Blade suggested.

Nodding, she walked over to pick up her tote bag with the cute gray bear peeking out from the top. "The manager will be here any minute to go through the apartment. Could we wait for her?"

"Of course."

"Knock, knock," Sara, from the management office, called from the doorway.

"Hi, Sara. Come in. We've gotten everything moved," Sapphire told her.

"And all cleaned up. Maybe I should hire those hunky bikers helping you," Sara said, chuckling.

"I was afraid you'd get some calls about the invasion," Sapphire confessed.

"Just a few. It was obvious to everyone quickly that they weren't here to rumble," the manager said. "I'll just do a fast round of the apartment and see if there's any damage."

"Of course," Sapphire told her.

In a few minutes, Sara had finished her inspection and double-checked she had Sapphire's new contact information to send a refund of her deposit. "We'll miss having you as a tenant. I'll have to come down to The Blue Door to do some shopping soon."

"I'd love to see you, Sara," Sapphire assured her as they all walked out together.

They parted ways at the door. Blade escorted Sapphire to his bike and securely fastened the tote bag in one of his saddlebags before lifting her helmet from the seat.

"Let's get this on, Blue Eyes." He fit the protective device on her head and pulled the strap securely before straightening the blue fuzzy ears. "You look adorable."

Sapphire reached up to stroke the new attachments. She loved them so hard. "Thank you for my ears."

"You totally needed those." He tilted her chin up and kissed her warmly. "Let's go home."

"Yes, Daddy."

Blade strapped on his helmet and straddled his bike. His movements shouldn't have turned her on, but they did. *I've got it bad.*

When he had the motor running and the bike balanced between his powerful thighs, Blade waved to her to mount behind him. Sliding into place, Sapphire hugged his trim waist and scooted as close as possible.

He wrapped a hand around her thigh and squeezed before grabbing his handlebar. In seconds, he glided smoothly from the parking spot. She closed her eyes and rested her head on his back, savoring the feel of him against her. Riding with Blade was exciting. Between the throb of the motor between her legs and the excuse to hold on to his hard body, Sapphire enjoyed every trip.

Opening her eyes, she appreciated the scenery on their route. Sapphire sat up straight when Blade drove past the clubhouse. Leaning close to his ear, she called, "Where are we going?"

"It's a surprise, Little girl."

"Don't we need to help unload?" she worried.

"No. The guys have it."

Arguing on a motorcycle wasn't feasible. Sapphire decided Blade knew his MC brothers better than she did. She wouldn't worry about offending them.

She relaxed and enjoyed the drive. It was the perfect day. Not too hot, not too cold. The sky was gorgeous with a few wispy clouds.

When Blade slowed to take a small dirt path, she squeezed him a bit tighter. This was her first time off a paved road. They bounced along, turning several times until a crystal blue lake appeared beside them. Blade circled around it and finally brought the bike to a stop at a small cabin next to the water.

When he switched off the engine, she asked, "Where are we?"

"This is Shadow Lake. It runs along one side of Shadowridge. A client of mine owns this house. His family isn't able to use the cabin often. I have a standing invitation to visit."

"It's lovely."

"We're both hot and sweaty from moving. I thought you might enjoy going swimming," Blade suggested.

"Really? I don't have a suit," she said, worried.

"I never do. It's isolated. No one will make their way here without us seeing them coming."

"Skinny dipping? I haven't done that since I was a teenager."

"Sounds like you've waited long enough. Slide off. Let's go grab some towels from the porch."

Sapphire dismounted. Blade joined her and took her hand, squeezing it gently. "Come on, Blue Eyes."

All her reservations disappeared. There was no way Blade would ever put her at risk. Going swimming sounded divine. She grinned at him. "You have such good ideas."

"Last one in is a rotten egg," he challenged, tugging her toward the water. Along the way, he dropped the towels on a grassy spot before reaching over his head to pull off his T-shirt.

Feeling daring at the sight of Blade undressing, Sapphire stepped out of her shoes. It had been a long time since she'd done something this carefree. Her shirt was next.

She loved the heat in his eyes as he took in her lacy blue bra. It had been dangerously expensive, but the attention she got now made it totally worth it. Sapphire shimmied out of her tight jeans to reveal the matching panties. Blade immediately walked forward to run his hands over her arms as he got a closer look.

"Fuck, Little girl. You dressed up for me," he growled.

"I thought I'd take advantage of you being distracted with organizing the move." Sapphire had jumped into the fancy underclothes when Steele had called Blade from the apartment.

With him out of the room, she'd plotted a surprise. She just hadn't expected it to happen here.

Shivering as he ran a finger over the decorative edge, Sapphire asked, "Do you like it?"

"No. It needs to come off," Blade ordered.

"Would you help me with that?" Her fluttering eyelashes added a compelling touch.

Blade didn't hesitate. He traced the band under her breasts, allowing the tops of his fingers to graze over the sensitive underside. She froze as he deftly unhooked the garment. Stroking his palms along the slight indent in her skin from the clasp around to the front, Blade slid his fingers under the lace to ease the material from her skin.

"You're so beautiful, Little girl. You don't need fancy underthings to keep my attention, but you make a fun package to open," he told her softly as he rubbed a fingertip over her taut nipples.

"I like to open packages too," she teased him, running the back of her hand over the bulge growing in his jeans.

"Help Daddy."

That permission to touch him was all she needed. Sapphire would try everything she wanted to do and see where he stopped her. Her fingers flew down the buttons of his jeans, unfastening them and allowing his heavy shaft to spring out. Dropping to her knees, she coaxed his jeans over his muscular butt after pressing a line of kisses along his length.

Blade shifted to grab one of the towels. He arranged it on the grass near his feet. "Come here, Blue Eyes."

She scrambled the short distance to kneel in front of him. Running her fingers along his erection, she peeked up at him, waiting for permission.

"Let me feel your lips on my cock."

Leaning forward, she wrapped one hand around him. She tasted the broad head. His groan made her smile as she swirled her tongue over him repeatedly. Sliding his tip into her mouth,

Sapphire slowly bobbed her head, working him deeper. Blade's hands tangled in her hair, urging her on and delivering a faint sting of pain. She loved knowing she tested his control.

Sapphire took him in as far as she dared, his length and girth challenging her. She wrapped her hand around the thick base and squeezed as she pulled back, keeping the suction strong all the way to the tip.

"Fuck, Sapphire. Your mouth is talented. Take me deep."

Of course, she followed his instructions. She loved his taste. This felt like a dream. Here all alone in this beautiful spot, she had his full attention. Sapphire tried to push her limits, but Blade's hands tightened in her hair, stopping her.

"I love how you take me into your mouth, Sapphire. I don't want to hurt you."

She swallowed and heard him moan. He liked that. Sapphire had read about that move in one of the books in the Littles' library at the clubhouse. The Daddy in that story had enjoyed it a lot. She tried it again.

"Damn, you're going to make me come like a fourteen-year-old boy. I need you to orgasm first, Little girl."

Blade stepped back and got rid of his pants fully before holding out his hand. She stared at him hard. "I was having fun."

"Me, too, sweetheart. I thought we could have some fun together."

After considering that, she reached up and allowed Blade to tug her to stand in front of him.

"Water or here?" he asked.

"Can we do that?" she asked. Sapphire had never made love in anything wetter than the shower.

"Oh, yeah. Come on, Blue Eyes. Race you to the edge."

It only took her a second to realize he had gotten a head start. Sapphire sprinted after him, enjoying the sight of his nude body moving so athletically. She'd almost caught up to him when he splashed into the lake.

"It was a tie," he judged, hugging Sapphire to his torso as he backed into the cool liquid.

"Brrr!" Her breasts were not pleased when they reached water high enough to lap over her chest.

"It will get better. Come here," Blade said, pulling her close.

His heat was magnificent. Sapphire wrapped herself around him. "Oh, you feel so good."

"Just wait, Little girl."

Blade caressed her with his hands. The sensation of him stroking her with the satiny water made her heat up quickly. She risked easing her hold around his neck. When she didn't slide under the water but stayed easily in place with her legs still wrapped around his waist, Sapphire had fun touching him as well. Tracing the grooves in his muscular chest, she explored his hard form as the water rocked her toward him.

His hands cupped her bottom. He fitted her pussy to his erection and firmly rubbed her against him, bringing a groan to both their lips.

"Kiss me, Sapphire."

Abandoning her play, she tilted her mouth toward him. When he didn't press his mouth to hers, she wrapped her fingers through his hair and pulled him close. Touching her lips to his softly at first, Sapphire deepened the kiss. Blade hugged her tightly as if she were the most delectable treat he'd ever tasted.

The heat grew in her lower abdomen. Sapphire bounced tentatively, rubbing her body on Blade's thick shaft. Enjoying that way too much, she repeated the motion over and over. His hands supported her but allowed her to move exactly how she desired.

"Please. I need you inside me," she begged as the tension inside her grew to an unbearable level.

"Damn! That lingerie set knocked everything from my brain. I'll be right back."

Sapphire couldn't stop the giggles that bubbled through her lips as he helped her stand before dashing out of the water to grab a condom. She liked knowing she'd distracted him. The laughter didn't mute her arousal. It was fun. Sex didn't always have to be serious with Blade.

In a flash, he returned, sheathed in a condom and ready to go. Blade raised her so she could regain her position before boosting her slightly out of the water. "Fit me into your opening, Sapphire."

She reached a hand between them to align him. As soon as she placed the head of his cock at her entrance, Blade lowered Sapphire. He sank into her slowly as Blade's muscles bulged with strength. Never rushing her, he took his time to allow her tight channel to stretch around him until she rested against his hard body once more.

Sapphire experimented with her previous bouncing motion. The resulting sensations sent stars twinkling through her brain.

"Do it again," he growled, leaning forward to nibble along the sensitive cord of her neck.

Eagerly, Sapphire repeated her movement. She loved knowing that she could bring him pleasure. It was a powerful, sexy feeling. Blade was so focused on her enjoyment, she treasured attending to his desires as well.

Playfully splashing some water over his shoulders, she caressed his slick skin as their bodies crashed together. Blade's athletic form was like a playground for her touch. Everywhere she explored was a new favorite place to savor.

Losing track of everything around her, Sapphire's world narrowed down to the two of them. When Blade's teeth closed on that sensitive spot at the curve of her shoulder, it was the last sensation she needed to push her over the edge. With a cry, she allowed her climax to crash over her.

"Blue Eyes," he said hoarsely and sped up his thrusts into her. Her orgasmic spasms pushed his erection into a massive eruption inside her.

With them wrapped around each other, Sapphire could feel Blade's heart beating strongly. She smiled into the curve of his throat before leaning back to press sweet kisses to his mouth. His answering squeeze around her torso told her he celebrated having her in his life.

She lifted her lips from his and stared at his handsome face. To her delight, that strand of hair that always seemed to tumble over his forehead lay in that tempting spot. Sapphire reached up and swept it away as she had wanted to from the very beginning. Her heart skipped a beat as she realized how much she loved this man and how deep their relationship had become.

"My handsome Daddy," she whispered.

"Handsome and fierce, right?" he prompted, putting on his mean biker face. It conflicted completely with the tender way he held her in his arms.

"The fiercest Shadowridge MC member ever." She played along before giggling.

"And you, my chortling Little girl, you are simply the best gift I could have ever found. I'm never letting you go," Blade warned.

"I'm counting on that, Daddy."

Thank you for reading Blade: Shadowridge Guardians Book 10!

Don't miss future sweet and steamy Daddy stories by Pepper North? Subscribe to my newsletter!

I'm excited to offer you a glimpse into Drake: Fated Dragon Daddies Book 1, the steamy paranormal romance book that introduces a new series of dragon shifter daddies!

5.0 out of 5 stars
WOW!! So Absorbing!

Well written story and well developed characters. The book needs to grab me and keep me involved from the beginning and all the way to the end! This one does that very well! I can't wait to read the next one!

5.0 out of 5 stars
Fantastic first
Drake is a fantastic first in a new series. Dragon shifters finding their mates as the world is rapidly changing. I loved watching Drake and Aurora come together. I can't wait to see where the author takes us next.

Drake: Fated Dragon Daddies Book 1
Chapter One

Aurora quickly walked by the old cemetery. It wasn't that she was afraid of ghosts. She shied away from the activity happening there to give those visiting privacy. Today, a stream of people dressed in black occupied the place. With a glance, Aurora noted someone being buried in one of the old family plots. She shivered at the thought of being locked inside one of the stone mausoleums, even if her family had one.

All the founding families did. They'd established Wyvern centuries ago. The area was sheltered from marauders in a valley surrounded by mountains. Over the years, new settlers had added a ring of newer buildings around the oldest part of the city. It hadn't grown quickly and still held that small, lost-in-time feel.

Cut off from other cities by sheer distance and tricky roads, it was an odd combination of modern living and old-fashioned practices. There was a lot of history in the stone buildings that still formed the center of the town for those who appreciated it—or even stopped to notice the cobbled streets and beastly gargoyles forming the rain spouts of many of the oldest homes and stores.

Just back from finishing her four-year business degree in Dallas, Aurora hadn't been overjoyed to come home with her tail between her legs. She'd been so sure she'd get a job at the elite company she interned for during the summers that she hadn't explored other options. Turned out, the company didn't wish to offer her a position when she graduated, but preferred candidates with five or more years of experience.

She'd scrambled to apply elsewhere but everyone in her graduating class had gotten their applications in first. Aurora wished she had a hundred dollars for every interviewer who told her they wished she had applied earlier but all the positions were now filled. Then she would have been able to pay her rent for a few more months.

The whisper of a noise behind her made her turn. She jumped back at the sight of a stunningly handsome man standing right behind her. His hair was thick—jet black with streaks of silver. It looked slightly unkempt as if he had neglected to cut it for a while. She had the weirdest urge to reach forward and brush it from his eyes.

Clutching her skirt with her hands to avoid giving in to that temptation, Aurora couldn't look away. She shivered slightly at the scar that ran along his cheek. Faded into a white line, it didn't detract from his appeal but gave him a dangerous air, as did the scruffy beard from not shaving for several days. She did not want to mess with this man. Yet, she wondered how his beard would feel if they kissed.

He stretched out a hand and she automatically responded to his silent request. Letting go of the fabric, she placed her palm against his and watched her hand disappear as his powerful one closed around it. A fire flared in his blue eyes, turning them gold. She felt like he could see through her.

Disconcerted, Aurora tried to pull away. She panicked when a sharp heat built on the back of her hand. "You're hurting me," she cried as she tugged harder to free herself.

"I was not expecting to find you today," he said harshly. His statement almost sounded like a curse.
Frightened by his tone, Aurora yanked her hand, trying to free it. He held her effortlessly, not even budging with the force of her movement.

"You will learn that all things happen on my time, Aurora. The pain should be gone now," he commented in a deep voice that seemed to resonate within her.

To her surprise, he abruptly released her hand. She staggered back a few steps, looking at her hand for damage. It was fine. Not a single mark, bruise, or red spot marred her skin. Astonished, she looked up quickly and met his steely gaze.

Aurora was rattled to realize the sharp pain was not the only result of touching him. That reaction soon paled in comparison to a consuming arousal building deep inside her. She'd never felt an attraction like that to anyone. Frightened, Aurora turned and ran down the cobbled streets of the Old Town.

She looked back over her shoulder before turning the corner and found him still standing there watching her. Feeling as if she were physically dragging herself away, Aurora dashed to her car and threw herself inside. Driving away felt awful for a few blocks before the need to turn around ebbed slightly—still there, but less urgent.

The heat, however, didn't abate. All she could think about was getting home to spend time with her vibrator. A picture of the room she shared with her sister once again popped into her mind. Aurora shook her head. There simply was no privacy in the home she shared with her family. There would be no relief for her there.

Gritting her teeth, she continued driving. Her family's home was in the middle of the modernized section of Wyvern surrounding the oldest section of the city. Her grandparents still occupied the ancestral home in the Old Town. It was large and had many rooms for guests. They would welcome her to stay with them.

Making a decision quickly, Aurora pulled onto a side street and parked. She pulled her phone out of her purse and called her grandmother.

"Hi, Aurora. I'm so glad to hear from you. Have you changed your mind? Can I tempt you to come stay with us?"

"Hi, Grandma. Like always, you can read my mind. I think sometimes you know me better than I do."

"There is a tie between all the women of our lineage," her grandmother said knowingly.

Not knowing what to say to that, Aurora concentrated on her reason for calling. "I did call to see if I can live with you for a while. Just until I find a job. Then, I'm afraid I'll have to move away from Wyvern."

"There's plenty of time to worry about the future. I'm going to focus on today. Believe it or not, Madelyn freshened up the pink room for you today. I had a feeling you might be coming soon."

Aurora smiled. The crafty woman knew she loved the ruffles and lace in the beautiful room. "You are the best, Grandma. I'm going to go pack some things and I'll be there in a couple hours."

"We'll be glad to see you, sweetheart."

Smiling, Aurora disconnected the call and dropped her phone in her purse. She merged back into traffic. Her grandparents would hover and be interested in everything she did. Even as an adult, she'd need to be home by a reasonable hour. That wasn't a problem. She'd gotten burned out on partying in college and she definitely didn't have a boyfriend to spend the night with.

Just that thought of having sex made her hunch over slightly as the heat inside her flared. *What in the hell is going on?* She'd had sex before but didn't really understand the allure.

Sex was okay, but she'd never seen rockets bursting in the air. The guys she'd been with seemed to think it was her fault she hadn't orgasmed. Whatever they were doing seemed to work for other girls. Either she was weird in some way, or their previous partners had totally faked their orgasms. Aurora was betting the second one was the truth.

She pressed a hand low on her abdomen, trying to soothe the ache. Never had she felt anything like this, even at the beginning of a relationship when she'd been the most attracted to her boyfriend at the time. Maybe something was wrong.

Shaking her head at the mere thought of going to the doctor, she abandoned that plan. How in the world would she explain this feeling to a doctor? She'd go if it didn't get better in a few days. Maybe she just ate something that was off.

When she pulled up in the drive, her sister rushed out to
meet her.

"You can't put your stuff on my side of the room," Sheila
informed her as Aurora got out of the car.

"Sorry. I didn't mean to invade." Distracted by a thick tower of
black smoke at the top of one of the mountains surrounding the
city, she wondered if the fire would endanger Wyvern.

"And yet you always do," Sheila sneered, drawing her back into
the conversation. "Your laundry basket is one inch over in my
space."

"Yikes. I'll move it," Aurora promised. She knew her sister had
thoroughly enjoyed having the room to herself when Aurora had
gone to college. It was hard to lose that independence.
"Grandma called and I'm going to stay with them for a while."

"Really?" Sheila tried unsuccessfully to keep the excitement out
of her voice.

"Really. Try not to miss me too bad," Aurora urged, walking
inside and holding the door open for her sister.

"Why should she miss you?" Aurora's father, Carl, asked.

"She's going to stay at Grandma's," Sheila rushed to tell him.

"That's a great idea. They'll love to have you there," her father
said with a smile. "You do know you're always welcome here,
despite what your kid sister might have said."

"Hey! I didn't say anything," Sheila protested.

"Sheila's been great. It seemed like a good idea to spend time with Grandma and Grandpa before I move away for a job. They're not getting any younger," Aurora pointed out.

"They're going to be around for a while," her dad said with a laugh. "But I think you'll both enjoy having each other around." He didn't have to add, 'unlike your sister who's counting down the days until you leave.'

A flare of desire caught her by surprise, and she pressed a hand to her stomach.

"Ew! You're not getting sick, are you?" Sheila asked with all the drama a sixteen-year-old could muster.

"Nope. I'm good. I'll just go grab my stuff."

In the shared bedroom, she quickly packed clothes she would need for the next couple of weeks. She could always come back for more if she got tired of wearing them. Even under the watchful eye of her sister, she was able to get the one thing she needed most into her suitcase. She crossed her fingers that the vibrator would ease the need growing inside her.

When she picked up her childhood stuffie, Sheila made fun of her. "Don't you think it's time you gave up your stuffed animal? How many college graduates still sleep with one every night?"

"Firefly will be with me forever. Some friends are for life."

Aurora had known upon seeing the stuffie that he was hers. She'd always been a compliant child, not one who used tantrums to get her way. That day remained in her memory as clear as day. She could not leave without Firefly and had sat down in the middle of the aisle with the stuffie pressed to her heart. Finally, her father had given her an advance on her allowance to buy him. Aurora hadn't cared a bit about losing her spending money. Firefly was worth that and more.

Pushing her sister's teasing from her mind, Aurora checked her closet for anything else she needed to take with her. She ran through the things she knew she'd need. Jeans, check. Leggings, check. T-shirts, check. Underwear, check. *Hmmm, I might need some fancier clothes.*

Scrutinizing her choices, Aurora picked out a pair of slacks and a white button-down shirt. As a lark, she grabbed the short black cocktail dress she'd worn to bars. It was nice enough that if her grandparents had a dinner party she could dress for the event.

Walking out the front door, she lugged everything to her sensible sedan. All that remained was to hug everyone goodbye and make sure she had her charger.

"Hey, Dad. On my way out. Do you know where Mom is?" Aurora asked, bracing her hand on the leather recliner next to the twin that held her father.

"What's that on your hand?" he asked.
Bemused, she held out her right hand, palm up. Maybe he was going to give her some money. To her surprise, he turned it over to look at the normally smooth skin on top of her hand. There were some raised bumps on it. He stroked a finger over one small section.

"Eccch!" She yanked her hand away and slapped it over her mouth as a wave of overwhelming nausea almost made her throw up.

"I thought you said you weren't sick?" her sister taunted from the entrance to the hallway.

"Talk to my mom about your hand," her father said quietly. Looking more serious than she'd seen him before, he pulled Aurora into his arms and hugged her tightly before releasing her. "Go on. You can call your mom later and explain."

"Thanks, Dad."

Aurora fled through the front door and gulped fresh air desperately. The nausea abated quickly. Jumping into her car, she turned on the radio to distract herself and drove away. Maybe she was sick. Grandma would know what to do. She always knew.

Her eyes automatically went to the mountain in front of her. The smoke had lessened. Whatever it was, it looked like it would not be a threat now.

Want to read more? One-click Drake: Fated Dragon Daddies Book 1

Read more from Pepper North

Fated Dragon Daddies

Change is coming to Wyvern.
A centuries-old pact between the founders and their powerful
allies could save the inhabitants of the city once again, but only a
dragon Daddy can truly guard his mate from harm.

Shadowridge Guardians

Combining the sizzling talents of bestselling authors Pepper North, Kate Oliver, and Becca Jameson, the Shadowridge Guardians are guaranteed to give you a thrill and leave you dreaming of your own throbbing motorcycle joyride.

Are you daring enough to ride with a club of rough, growly, commanding men? The protective Daddies of the Shadowridge Guardians Motorcycle Club will stop at nothing to ensure the safety and protection of everything that belongs to them: their Littles, their club, and their town. Throw in some sassy, naughty, mischievous women who won't hesitate to serve their fair share of attitude even in the face of looming danger, and this brand new MC Romance series is ready to ignite!

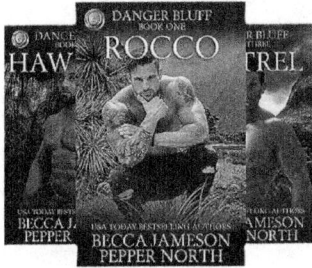

Danger Bluff

Welcome to Danger Bluff where a mysterious billionaire brings together a hand-selected team of men at an abandoned resort in New Zealand. They each owe him a marker. And they all have something in common–a dominant shared code to nurture and protect. They will repay their debts one by one, finding love along the way.

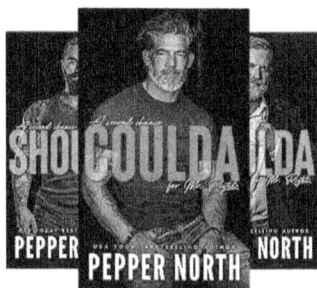

A Second Chance For Mr. Right

For some, there is a second chance at having Mr. Right. Coulda,
Shoulda, Woulda explores a world of connections that can't
exist... until they do. Forbidden love abounds when these Daddy
Doms refuse to live with regret and claim the women who own
their hearts.

Little Cakes

Welcome to Little Cakes, the bakery that plays Daddy matchmaker! Little Cakes is a sweet and satisfying series, but dare to taste only if you like delicious Daddies, luscious Littles, and guaranteed happily-ever-afters.

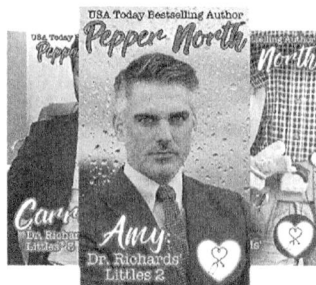

Dr. Richards' Littles®

A beloved age play series that features Littles who find their forever Daddies and Mommies. Dr. Richards guides and supports their efforts to keep their Littles happy and healthy.

Note: Zoey; Dr. Richards' Littles® 1 is available FREE on Pepper's website:
4PepperNorth.club

Dr. Richards' Littles®
is a registered trademark of
With A Wink Publishing, LLC.
All rights reserved.

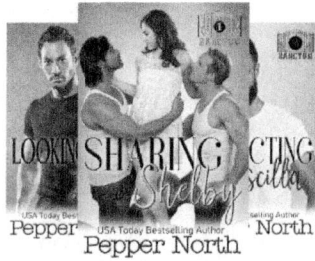

SANCTUM

Pepper North introduces you to an age play community that is isolated from the surrounding world. Here Littles can be Little, and Daddies can care for their Littles and keep them protected from the outside world.

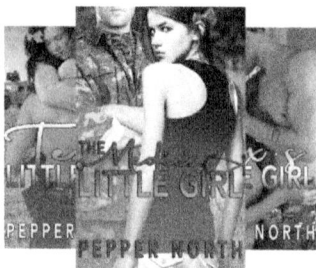

Soldier Daddies

What private mission are these elite soldiers undertaking?
They're all searching for their perfect Little girl.

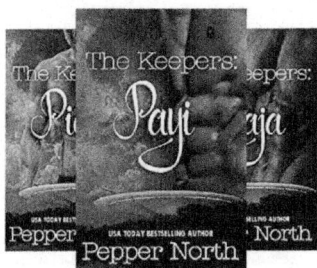

The Keepers

This series from Pepper North is a twist on contemporary age play romances. Here are the stories of humans cared for by specially selected Keepers of an alien race. These are science fiction novels that age play readers will love!

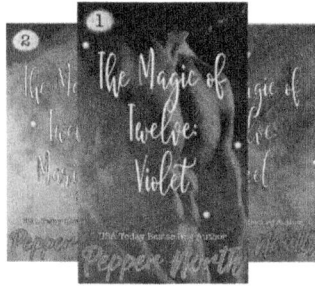

The Magic of Twelve

The Magic of Twelve features the stories of twelve women transported on their 22nd birthday to a new life as the droblin (cherished Little one) of a Sorcerer of Bairn. These magic wielders have waited a long time to take complete care of their droblin's needs. They will protect their precious one to their last drop of magic from a growing menace. Each novel is a complete story.

Ever just gone for it? That's what *USA Today* Bestselling Author Pepper North did in 2017 when she posted a book for sale on Amazon without telling anyone. Thanks to her amazing fans, the support of the writing community, Mr. North, and a killer schedule, she has now written more than 180 books!
Enjoy contemporary, paranormal, dark, and erotic romances that are both sweet and steamy? Pepper will convert you into one of her loyal readers. What's coming in the future? A Daddypalooza!

Sign up for Pepper North's newsletter

Like Pepper North on Facebook

Join Pepper's Readers' Group for insider information and giveaways!

Follow Pepper everywhere!

Amazon Author Page
BookBub
FaceBook
GoodReads
Instagram
TikToc
Twitter
YouTube
Visit Pepper's website for a current checklist of books!

Printed in Great Britain
by Amazon